W9-COB-737

The Children of the Cave

The Children of the Cave

A TALE OF ISRAEL AND OF ROME

ZVI LIVNE

English translation by Zipora Raphael

HENRY Z. WALCK, INC. NEW YORK

Livne, Zvi
The children of the cave; a tale of Israel and of Rome; tr. by Zipora Raphael. Walck, 1970
218p.

First pub. in England in 1969.
Dramatic story of the children who survived slaughter by conquering Romans in A.D. 70.

1. Palestine - History - Fiction
I. Title

Note

As the Hebrew calendar is based on lunar months, the English equivalents to the Jewish months are only approximate. *Kislev* roughly corresponds to December, *Shvat* to March, *Tevet* to January and *Tishrei* to September.

Standard Book Number: 8098-3087-6
Library of Congress Catalog Card Number: 76-100707
Printed in the United States of America

Contents

PART ONE

THE REVOLT

1

Down on the mountain slope, near the valley, roves a small herd of goats. It is five o'clock in the afternoon. The goats leap from rock to rock, graze a little, and then leap again.

Next to a carob tree stands a boy of about twelve, with a staff in one hand. He plays on a flute. His eyes are large, dreamy and yet full of daring. His head is crowned with curls above his sunburned face. His face tells of strength of character, of cleverness. His name is Avshalom, son of Abraham. The herd is his father's herd and he is its shepherd. As he plays his flute, he hears the sound of approaching footsteps. He finishes his tune, turns and listens, and above, from the fig orchard, comes a voice—sweet, clear, childish.

"Avshalom! Avshalom!"

Avshalom's face lights up and he shouts, "Rachel! Rachel! Here I am!"

Like a gazelle, a little girl of eleven comes nimbly down the slope. She is black-haired, black-eyed, suntanned, barefoot. A red ribbon on her hair enhances her charm. Avshalom reaches out his hand to greet her and the two run down after the straying herd.

In her other hand, Rachel has a bunch of grapes, and after they retrieve the herd, they sink to the ground, tired, panting, and Rachel holds up the grapes and smiles: "Open your mouth, and I'll give you a drink of grape juice." Avshalom opens his mouth wide, and Rachel pops the grapes, one by one, into his mouth. They laugh gaily and unrestrainedly—childish laughter. But suddenly Rachel's face darkens. She holds Avshalom's hand tightly, and in a trembling voice, falters: "Avshalom, have you heard?"

Her friend turns to her, sees how sad she has suddenly become and is afraid.

"What has happened, Rachel? Tell me."

"The Romans are coming nearer. Menachem has returned, and, with him, a fugitive from the north, and they say the Romans are killing all who rise against them, destroying and burning the villages and towns of Galilee. Our villages may be threatened next. There's to be a meeting at sunset in the village. Some people want to fight, some want to give in to the Romans and wait for some change in the future."

Avshalom's eyes glint with anger. "We *must* resist!" he cries. "Better to die a hero's death than to live in slavery!"

Tears appear in Rachel's eyes. "Avshalom, Avshalom,

will you really be able to stand up to even the weakest among the Romans? They will kill you and . . ." She bursts out crying. He strokes her dark hair, wipes her tears, and whispers softly, "Don't be afraid, Rachel. God, the God of our Fathers, will come to our help. If I die, death is better than life without freedom."

2

The events of which I tell took place in the Year of Chastisement, A.D. 70, which so many generations have mourned, the year of the Destruction of Jerusalem and the Second Temple. Avshalom and Rachel live in the Land of Israel, which is under attack by mighty Rome–seeking to conquer all the known world. Although they live in a small isolated village, rumbles of the war reach them through occasional travelers and flying rumors. They know that the people of Israel are fighting courageously against their powerful enemy, who seeks to rob them of liberty, to trample underfoot all they hold sacred–the teachings of the Torah, the Laws of Moses, mercy and justice and morality.

The village of Vale-of-Figs is hidden among the hills. Around it are the lofty and steep ranges of the Mountains of Ephraim. It is tucked away, far from roads and highways, from other villages. Even its fields are hidden from view, as they lie in the well-watered valley below the western slope of the ridge on which the village nestles. On this slope grow the grapes, the olives, and the famed fig orchards which give the village its name. The other three sides of the ridge are covered with bare, gray rocks, the whole forbidding rugged aspect completely belying the existence of the village on the other side. Because it is cut off in this fashion, the Roman legions have been slow in coming to it, venting their anger instead on the villages of the plains and the towns on the highways. Great is the anger of Rome that a little country like Judah has dared to defy the Sledgehammer of the World. And in her anger is fear too that Judah's example may inspire revolts in other parts of the Empire.

But in the little village of Vale-of-Figs, there is by no means agreement as to how the villagers should act when the legions approach.

Avshalom and Rachel join the throng of villagers heading for the village square. Young and old hasten to hear the latest news from Menachem, one of the villagers who has just returned from a journey beyond the mountains to the Emek Yezreel, bringing with him a fugitive from Galilee.

"What news of Jerusalem and the siege? What news of the Holy City, the Temple?" come the questions from all sides.

"Jerusalem is still resisting the siege," Menachem begins. "Our youth everywhere form a living wall, fighting body and soul for the Motherland. But the Romans pour in thousands and thousands of soldiers to replace the thousands whom we have slain. Famine and pestilence stalk in the streets of Jerusalem. Rabbi Yochanan ben Zakkai, it is rumored, has escaped from the city and has gathered pupils at Yavneh to keep the Torah safe."

"What of the north? What news from Galilee?"

"Tiberias has fallen," reports Menachem, "and has been utterly destroyed. Yes, Trichia is in ruins, although the Zealots there defended it with acts of breath-taking courage. They say two hundred and fifty old people were put to death, while thousands of young people were sold as slaves. In Gamla, too, the Romans took savage revenge for the resistance of the Zealot heroes Yosef and Charash. There they held out for months under siege. All the townsmen were slaughtered, and only two girls remained alive to tell the tale."

The people sit hushed, their flesh rising in goose pimples, the children all ears as they crowd at the travelers' feet.

"Woe is me!" cries the fugitive from Galilee. "The fortresses Yodfat and Yofia have fallen too, and are annihilated, the men slain, the women tortured and the strong sold into serfdom. Yosef, son of Matityahu, ruler of Tiberias, who defended Yodfat, has fled. No one knows if he has been killed or if he still lives. It is even whispered that he has become a traitor and gone over to the Romans. Many villages have surrendered. Zealots who are conquered are slaughtered publicly and those escaping alive have scattered like chaff, some to Jerusalem, some to Gush-Halav. I myself got away by a miracle."

"What of the town of Zippori?" asks Uziah, the village elder, a judge and a man of substance.

Zippori surrendered so the Romans did no damage there."

"Then there were no Zealots there?" asks Uziah again.

"I heard it said there were but a few. The Moderates, who were the majority, were too quick for them, and came to an agreement with the Romans before the Zealots could fortify the town and seize power."

"What are you?" asks Abraham, Avshalom's father. "Zealot or Moderate?"

"I am a farmer, a tiller of the soil. At first I thought the Zealots were right and followed them, for how can we let the Romans enslave us and rob us of liberty? But now I am not sure. I don't know what to think. What does a mere farmer know?" He heaves a great sigh. "All I know is that my possessions have been plundered. Nothing is left of my village near Yofia. Some were killed. Others dispersed like me."

As he says this, he weeps bitterly, covering his face with his cloak, so that even the bystanders tremble, stirred to the depths of their souls.

Uziah shakes his white head emphatically, and his eyes blaze with anger as he cries: "Here you see what comes of the Zealots' puerile actions! Here is the result of the revolt which the impetuous advocate! Because of their irresponsibility, a beautiful town has been destroyed and many people murdered. It is not fitting for Judah, poor little Judah, to swell up like a toad and brag, 'I am an elephant!' "

Many heads nod in agreement. At the same time there is

a rumble of dissent from those who oppose surrender, whose hatred of tyranny burns fiercely in their breasts.

"Woe to the nation ruled by its boys!" cries Uziah. "These Zealots–their fanaticism is destroying the land and its people!"

Then a man of impressive stature, some thirty years of age, rises to his feet, his black eyes flashing. This is Yehudah the Shibbolite, known in the village as a quiet, industrious farmer, little involved in public affairs. "No!" he cries in a great voice. "Those who urge a shameful peace are the ones who have brought this distress upon us! Had we all risen together and gone out to war, we would have strangled the cruel serpent!"

Astonished, all turn their heads to look at Yehudah, usually so retiring. Uziah sits open-mouthed at this lack of respect for his opinion.

"These Romans begin with taxes and with levies," Yehudah continues passionately, "and then they buy kings and priests with their money. They provoke civil strife. They bring their barbarous customs with them. They will put idols in the Temple, and weaken Judah, in body and in spirit, so we will be assimilated and lost from the face of the earth!" Then, his voice ringing out loudly over the silent crowd, he cries, "This very night I shall go out to war in the sacred cause. Whoever wants to join me must come with me now!"

A great commotion arises, as voices burst out in confusion and words clash in a chaotic tangle. Uziah beats with his thick rod on the stone in front of him for silence. Then he speaks, accentuating each word by beating on the rock as though counting coins: "My brethren! I am like you. I feel as you do. Your spirits have been shaken at hearing the audacious words spoken by a good, upright man, by the Shibbolite; but his words have the spirit of evil in them. Woe to us if the plague of revolt infects us, for nothing is more bitter than its end! Rome is the conqueror of the world and states fall before her mighty armies like corn before the scythe. It seems to be God's decree that they should be rulers of the land and the sea. But great nations rise and fall, and the day of Rome too will pass. True, they install prefects and levy taxes, but they do not rob people of their lands; they permit the worship of God, and even grant self-rule. Let us accept the decree of God, and not be as the cedar, which does not bend before the storm and is uprooted, but rather as the reed which bends with the wind, and, when the storm abates, straightens itself once more. The Shibbolite is dear to us, but dearer still is truth. We shall go on working our vineyards, our fields, and if the Romans come to us, we shall go out to meet them, our hands held out in peace, and so our lives will be spared."

When he has finished speaking, all turn in the direction of Yehudah. But he is not to be seen. It is as though he has vanished.

Suddenly a young man of about twenty jumps up. It is Yochanan, orphaned of both father and mother, a man on his own. At first his speech is halting, but as he speaks, his tone becomes stronger. Then, like a hammer striking stone, he cries: "Jerusalem and the Temple are under siege. The pride of the sons of Judah are defending every hill, every rock, in the name of freedom. They use sword and spear, spade and scythe, sticks and stones. They make tools of peace into weapons of war. Shall we sit here, tranquil, each under his own vine and fig, and work our fields, and greet the Romans with welcoming faces? No! Yehudah the Shibbolite is right! Everyone who values freedom must leave his fields and his vineyards and must join the rebels to fight the violators of the world, of Judah! I am for Yehudah the Shibbolite, and I hope with all my heart that God in His Heaven will open the eyes of every one of you, so that each man will find the courage to go to war!"

As Yochanan finishes speaking, three other farmers stand up, also young men. But what they have to say is quite different. The dispute continues till after midnight, some on one side, some on the other, with tempers fiery and flaming, and words sharp as spurs. The Moderates, led by Uziah, are aghast that their remote village should be swept up in the tempest of revolt. Opposed to them are the Extremists. But there are not only Moderates and Extremists, there are also those who waver from one side to the other. When Uziah makes his points, they nod their heads in agreement, but when one of the impassioned supporters of the revolt stands up and speaks, again they nod in agreement.

At a late hour, when the leaders are hoarse from arguing, one of those who is neither hot nor cold, whispers to his friend: "I have to get up early to plow the field. Let's go."

As he speaks, two of them get up and leave, and then others steal away after them, and the crowd disperses of itself, until only the most adamant wranglers remain to continue the debate.

Avshalom turns to Rachel. "Yehudah is right. I wish he would take me with him!"

"But how can we stand against them? Perhaps Uziah is right? What will I do if a Roman attacks me? I'll be lost!"

Avshalom stops her angrily. "I'll chop him in two!" he declares.

3

Evening. Shulamit, the wife of Yehudah the Shibbolite, stands at a small, open fire in the yard, cooking in a large pot, stirring the food with a wooden spoon. She adds salt, and tastes the broth. She is a tall, slim woman, with long plaits curling behind her, and around her hips is a wide sash. She is twenty-five, but seems much younger.

Yehudah returns home from the meeting, stormy and agitated, but when he sees Shulamit bending over the fire, his anger subsides. Not a word does he address to her. He sits on the rush mat spread near the fig tree. She looks at him and says, "You must be hungry. Wait a little and we'll eat."

"No–I do not feel hungry. Sit here, my dear, next to me." She sits down and looks apprehensively into his eyes.

"What has happened, Yehudah?"

"Oh, nothing. We were sitting in the village square and discussing the war with the Romans."

Trembling, she asks: "Is the news bad? Tell me, tell me the truth. I can sense something terrible has happened."

"Menachem has returned, and with him a fugitive. They were full of hard tidings. Gamla has fallen. Tiberias, Trichia, Gamla, and all the neighboring villages are rivers of blood. The Kinneret is red with blood. Tens of thousands of young men have been sold as slaves, and sent to distant lands, and the old men, who were no good for any work, have been slaughtered like sheep. The defenders of the last fortress performed wonders, and yet, in the end, it was conquered. The vengeance of the Romans has been terrible. They have not left one person alive."

So saying, he sighs deeply, and falls silent. After a while, with a sudden movement, he clenches his fists. "But it is not with them that I am angry. My wrath burns against Agrippa, son of our Kings, whose soul is the soul of a slave, bought by the Romans! Who now sits in their camp, advising them and helping them, the traitor!"

He is silent for a while and then continues: "Treachery like this is consuming us. Look at Uziah, our honored, respected leader. He too is for surrender, for subjection!"

The pupils of Shulamit's eyes gleam in the darkness. Suddenly she flings back her left plait, which has strayed to her breast, raises her head high and cries, "Submission is despicable, and slavery even more despicable. Liberty or death!"

He throws his arms around her in a loving embrace, and after a while asks, "Shulamit, my sword—where is it?"

Shulamit goes pale. Two emotions clash in her breast—her fears for her husband, and the love of her people. She bites her lips, masters her emotion, and asks quietly: "Will you join the Zealots?"

"Yes."

She bends toward him, takes hold of his hand and lays her head on his chest. She whispers, trembling:

"Parting is hard but what can we do when the enemy has left us no alternative?" And, as she speaks, she bursts into tears. The silence which follows lasts only a few moments, but seems to Yehudah an eternity.

At last he says: "Dear Shulamit, I am causing you a great deal of sorrow, but what can I do? All the work will fall on you, and the longing, and looking after Gideon. But these are not normal times."

Shulamit gets up and looks at him, and her eyes are wet. "Yes, it will be hard to part, but I know I must not hold you back. If I had been a man, I too would have been one of those going into battle. Be strong and of good courage, my Yehudah, and may the God of Abraham, Isaac and Jacob guard you from all harm."

So engrossed are they in their talk that at first they do not notice a figure who comes and stands beside them. When they see him at last, Yehudah says: "Yochanan! Sit down!"

"Have you eaten yet?" Yochanan asks.

"No. We were talking."

Shulamit goes back to the fire and says: "Eat with us, Yochanan."

"Thank you. I wanted to talk to you, Yehudah!"

Shulamit spreads a white cloth on the mat, places on it bread, onions and salt, and serves the pottage of groats in wooden bowls.

Yochanan dips a crust in the salt, puts it into his mouth, and says: "I want to go with you, Yehudah."

"Just the two of us?"

"There may be another three who will join us."

"Five altogether. It is not an army. But maybe in these days that may turn out to be an advantage!"

Shulamit hardly touches her food. The men eat and talk. Quietly she brings them dates and pressed figs after the pottage. She asks: "What will you do?"

Yochanan looks at Yehudah, waiting for him to answer the question. Yehudah takes a single date in his hand, studying it as though it were a map, and says:

"Maybe I'll go to the camp of fighters on Mount Tabor. Maybe I'll go farther."

While he is still talking, two young men appear and Avshalom dashes in behind them, a bag on his back. "Take me with you, Yehudah," he shouts.

Yehudah ruffles Avshalom's dark hair, pinches his cheek lightly and looks fondly into his eyes. "Yes, I can see you'll be a valiant man. Your eyes tell of understanding and good sense. How old are you?"

"Twelve years old!"

"A real youth, I declare. But still a little small to fight against a Roman legionary." To the two young men he says, "Welcome, Yaacov. Welcome, Zakkai."

"We are going with you," they say.

"Are there any others from the village who will join us?"

"Possibly Shmuel, the Danite. He has gone to consult his wife first."

Avshalom persists: "Not all the fighting has to be hand to hand. You will need eyes to watch the Romans. What better, say, than a little shepherd boy, looking after his sheep and playing on his flute?"

Yehudah thinks hard for a few moments.

"Very well, if your parents agree, you can come," he says. "Now listen. With the dawn, I am leaving alone, not as a man of war, but as a farmer, with my staff in my hand, and figs for sale in my bag. I shall roam around for several days, and try to get near the enemy's camp. I'll look into every nook and cranny, and I'll hear what people are saying. Maybe I'll come across a few young men to join us. When I return, I'll tell you what I have heard and seen, and then we'll decide what course to take. Meanwhile, get yourselves ready. The Romans are heavily armed, properly clothed and shod. We don't need all that. The more lightly we're clad, the more easily we'll tread. But the little clothing we have must be stout and in good condition, not a shoelace frayed, nor a garment torn. And each one of you prepare your weapons, and have them in first-class condition."

They talk a little longer. Then the young men leave. "Yehudah, you won't forget about me?" Avshalom pleads, as he goes.

"Surely not," Yehudah replies, as he lies down to sleep for an hour or two. At daybreak he sets out on his way.

4

Yehudah wanders from place to place. He finds whole villages completely destroyed. The fields are desolate, the houses burned or torn down. Not a living soul is to be seen. Even in the villages which surrendered and are undamaged there is great depression; some of the young men have left to join the Zealots, some have been killed, some sold as slaves. Travel is difficult and dangerous. It seems the cruel hand of Rome is destroying the very marrow of life. News filters through from conquered Jaffa of Vespasian's cruel treatment of captives; from Jerusalem, too, come reports that strike despair into every Jewish heart.

All the villages through which Yehudah passes are split, with the Zealots on one side, and the Moderates on the other. In the villages which submitted to Rome, the Moderates prevail. The majority of the young Zealots have long since left them to join the heroes of Galilee. As for those who remain in the villages, every word they utter is suspect by the ruling power, especially as slander is rife. There are still some young men who go secretly to the villages and put spirit into the people, but somehow, the Roman envoys learn about them, and catch them. They are killed as rebels against the State.

Yehudah, who knows all this, is very cautious. He says little, but he is all ears, listening, listening, listening. Inside, he is like a fuming volcano of red-hot lava, but on the outside, it is as though events do not touch him at all, neither exciting nor depressing him. From the scraps of rumors, he gathers that two fortresses have not surrendered, one at Mount Tabor, and the other at Gush-Halav. He considers going to join the men on Mount Tabor—and then a bitter rumor reaches him that Mount Tabor too has been conquered. He hears the story.

For some months the Romans besieged this fortress, which is at the top of a high mountain. The defenders were valiant fighters. When the Romans saw that they could not take the fortress, they devised a trick. They began to flee as though conquered. The defenders of the fortress watched the flight of the enemy, and they came down to pursue the Romans with much shouting and rejoicing. But when the Romans had covered the distance of a mile or two, and their pursuers had come down to the plains, they turned around, fell upon their pursuers, and defeated them.

For a few days, Yehudah wanders in the forests in utter despair. He does not know what to do. It is clear to him that the Romans are installing themselves as rulers step by step. Finally, he determines to go on to the end, whatever it may be. He decides not to go as far north as Gush-Halav, nor as far south as Jerusalem. He will stay where he is. Here he will bind together a small group which will torment the Romans in various ways, for in open battle there is no chance of defeating the enemy, and therefore they will have to use cunning. Never will he permit the glowing embers of rebellion to be quenched; he will guard those last sparks of the fire of the Zealots; for he believes that if these sparks are not snuffed out, in the end they will flare up into a great flame which will envelop the enemy. Only thus will the Romans be driven from the country.

In the group that Yehudah forms, there are eight men, five from Vale-of-Figs and three from the lonely shepherd tents in the mountains. But the band numbers nine warriors—the ninth is Avshalom who has managed to persuade his parents to allow him to serve his country as Yehudah's eyes and ears.

There are some people who derive personal gain in war. They approach the Romans and negotiate with them. They supply foodstuffs, flour, fruit, vegetables, meat, milk. These people travel through the villages, buying what they can and passing their purchases on to the two Roman camps near Haifa and Yokneam for good prices.

All this Yehudah discovers by thoroughly exploring the whole area, with its villages, hills and valleys. He works out what methods his band should use, and what actions it should take. To Avshalom and the other shepherds, he says: "You will be shepherds of small flocks in the environs of the camps, and, apparently in all innocence, you will go with your flocks into the area surrounding the Romans. Pretend to be very simple. Keep your eyes open. See what they're doing. And listen to everything they say!"

Yehudah himself becomes a peddler buying eggs, fowls and fruit, and bringing them to the camp, where he proffers his wares. Thus he comes almost every day to one or other of the Roman camps. He sells some goods, sits down to rest for a while, negotiates again, his sharp eyes spying every movement and action, his ears taking in every sound. He even learns a little of the Roman language, and manages to talk with them. Occasionally, in great secrecy, he buys a sword or a spear from an irresponsible Roman soldier.

Thus Yehudah gets to know what is being discussed in the Roman camp. He learns that in a few days they will celebrate the birthday of the Emperor and that on that day good food and wine are to be handed out to the army. The soldiers ask him to get them some liquors and wines for the occasion and Yehudah quickly returns with ten camels loaded with skin bottles of very potent wine.

On the eve of the holiday, three of his comrades "happen" to appear near the camp, where they rest their camels at the spring. Yehudah is already there, selling eggs and fruit. He drops a hint to the Roman soldiers that the travelers have plenty of liquor in their saddlebags.

The Romans crowd around them, shouting, "Wine! Wine!" A few pay for the wine; others seize it, declaring, "Jews are nothing, and their wine is for nothing!"

Skin bottle after skin bottle they snatch, pour the wine into their own vessels and begin drinking.

This casual drinking lasts until evening. Then the official

drinking begins, with toasts of "Long life to Caesar and to Rome!" By midnight, they are all rolling drunk. Soon they are snoring. From out of the darkness creep the cloaked men, sharp Roman swords in their hands. The drunken soldiers pay a fearful price for their wine, for their cruelty to the Jews, for the Roman onslaught on liberty.

As silently as shadows, the cloaked men steal away.

The next morning, hundreds of Romans are found slain.

Learning that a new legion of Romans is about to arrive in the area, Yehudah plans a new stratagem. His shepherds, among them Avshalom, report that the legion will come in from the north, from the direction of Syria; they will cross through Tiberias, spend one night in the mountains around Nazareth, and the next day, by noon or by evening will reach the camp.

It is close to sunset. The Roman legion, numbering about fifteen hundred men, is marching along wearily, approaching the place where they are to sleep. The officer riding at their head suddenly notices a Roman soldier lying face down on the ground. "He is dead or unconscious," he thinks. He stops the soldiers marching behind him, dismounts and stoops over the soldier. He sees that he is not dead, but wounded and unconscious. The soldiers throw water on him and bring him around, his face injured, his clothes soaked in blood. They storm him with questions. From his answers, they learn that he is serving in one of the legions of reinforcements, which include men from Sidon, Syria, Egypt. He himself is a Syrian. Speaking the language of the Romans with difficulty, he stammers out that his officer sent him and another soldier to the camp of Acre. On their way, a band of Jews ambushed them, almost killing him, while the other man took to his heels and escaped. After hearing the wounded man's story, the Romans give him a drink, put him in a cart and move on their way.

Later, exhausted from their long march, they reach the camp. They sleep heavily, only the sentries standing on guard remain awake. They march along their beats, peer into the darkness, and listen to the noises of the night.

The wounded soldier—in reality Yehudah the Shibbolite—rises from the spot where he is supposed to be sleeping, crawls up to one of the sentries, and pulls out a small jug of wine. He appears to take a long drink, and then offers the jug to the sentry. The sentry drinks some of the wine. In a few moments drowsiness seizes him. Yehudah goes on to the next sentry and "shares" his wine with him as well. Eventually all the guards are stretched out, sunk in deep sleep.

When the moon sets, and only the stars twinkling above give out a little light, Yehudah strikes stone upon stone, causing a spark, from which he lights a small torch. His comrades see this sign, and come out of their hiding places on the nearby hill. Seven youths, wearing Roman uniforms, move silently through the camp, slaying Romans as they had done on the Emperor's birthday.

The next morning, when many of the Romans are found dead, panic strikes the camp. The Romans go to endless trouble to catch the partisans, but in vain. "These killers are ghosts, not men!" the more superstitious among them say.

Amid the Mountains of Ephraim, near Caesarea, is a large village, which surrendered to the Romans, but soon the newly inspired youths of the village rise and rebel against the Romans. They collect others like themselves from villages round about, fortify one village strongly, accumulate great stores of food, enough for a year, and prepare to resist. The village is situated at the summit of a high mountain. Below is a long, narrow valley, some miles distance from the Valley of Yezreel, on the road leading to Caesarea. The place is a natural fortress, and is the center of the neighboring villages, which are also fortified.

Yehudah maintains contact with these villages, keeping them informed of events in the area and in the Roman camp. He still enters the Roman camp as a trusted trader to sell wares, and secretly to buy weapons from the dishonest among them. His knowledge of their language improves, and he even makes friends among the Romans, from whom he receives important pieces of information.

One day, when he brings food to the camp, the cook says to him: "I want only half the quantity today that I buy usually." Yehudah pretends to be upset, and begins to wail: "Woe is me! My goods will be spoiled! What has happened to your people? Are they on a fast?"

"Far from it," replies the cook. "They are the same old gluttons as ever."

Yehudah keeps complaining: "If you won't buy my goods today, will you buy them tomorrow?"

"No. Half the army is leaving here."

Yehudah says, "I sincerely hope they'll come back, and buy my goods."

"No, no," says the cook. "They won't come back, but where they're going is a dark secret and I am not allowed to tell you."

Yehudah understands that the purpose of the move is important; either the Romans are preparing for battle, or for reprisals to punish rebels. He has to know which is correct. He begins to plead: "My dearly beloved friend! Look at these vegetables that are going to rot! Look at this fruit that is going to ruin! I've been your good friend all this time. Have pity on me, and give me just a hint where they're going, and I'll go there to sell them my goods. I'll even give you part of my profit!"

As he speaks, he takes money out of his belt, as if playing with it. The cook, understanding the hint, winks broadly. He bends down and whispers something in Yehudah's ear. He adds loudly: "But don't say a word. We've strict orders not to disclose the name of the new camp."

Yehudah is anxious to leave, but he maintains his casual expression. He remains in the camp for a little while longer, talking to one man and another. At last he leaves, as calmly as if he does not know what it means to hurry.

Yehudah reaches the threatened village about an hour and a half before sunset. He gives the password to the guard at the entrance to the village. Then he says in a commanding voice: "Take me at once to your leader. I have an important message for him."

"And who are you, rider?"

"I am Yehudah the Shibbolite."

"Yehudah the Shibbolite!" exclaims the guard in astonishment and with great respect. "At once, friend!"

Not ten minutes later, in the lofty stone building from the roof of which the entire area can be seen, the leader of the revolt rises to greet Yehudah. He is a short, stocky man, about thirty years of age, broad-shouldered, with stubbly hair and piercing eyes. His name in Yair, the Reubenite. He holds out his hand, horny and heavy.

"So you are Yehudah the Shibbolite! Blessed be thy coming. What news have you to comfort us with?"

The Shibbolite, exhausted after his furious riding, his throat parched, says: "Can I have some water, please? I am dying of thirst. I am afraid there is no comfort in my news. This very night half the Roman army encamped on the Carmel will set out and before morning they will be your guests. I have checked and rechecked this–and it is true."

Yair the Reubenite stands up, his eyes restless in their sockets. "Sit down, Yehudah," he says. "Soon they will bring you cold water, food and wine."

"This is not a time for feasting," says Yehudah impatiently. "We must decide on a plan. I am at your service."

The servant brings in a jug of water, wine, bread and olives. Yehudah drinks his fill. Then Yair asks: "How many are there?"

"Not less than a thousand men."

"We are well fortified. We have food for many days and we have a secret path to the spring on the slope of the mountains."

Yehudah gets up and paces the floor restlessly.

"And will you withstand a siege?"

"Yes, we'll let them besiege us. At the right moment, we'll break through and face them with sword and spear!"

"How many of your men have arms?"

"About two hundred and fifty fighting men. But there are also some old men who will defend the village, if need be."

"Listen to me, Reubenite. In the wood near here, my men await me. They number seven in all. The eighth is a boy whom we do not take into war. Give me forty more, or fifty, men of courage. We'll hide in the many caves opposite here, and attack the Romans from the rear."

It is clear from Yair's eyes that he is attracted by the plan, but shadow beclouds his face as he says: "How can we spare fifty of our best men? Where are the rest of your men?"

"My whole band is eight men."

"With only eight men you performed all the wonders we heard of?"

"Yes, they are all brave and strong and daring and quick, and know how to fling a shot."

The Reubenite gets up. "Your plan is excellent, but my men are too few. I'll try to collect men from the neighboring villages."

Yehudah stops pacing. His face is heavy and shows a small angry cloud of impatience.

"There is no time! Soon the sun will set. We have to find hiding places. We must prepare food and water for some days. We must arrange passwords and signals. Every moment we waste doing nothing spells great danger for us."

"You are right. Time is critical. Take twenty of my men.

Use them as you think fit. As leader of the group, I will give you a man who knows the paths around the villages very well. They say he can collect dozens of rebels in the area."

They confer for another half hour, and agree on passwords and signals.

Just as the sun sets, Yehudah disappears through the gates of the village.

5

It is not yet dawn when the scouts on the lookout become aware of movement in the vicinity. The feet of a thousand Romans draw nearer and nearer—tramp, tramp, tramp. The faces of the men on the wall darken. The war is coming. Even before the first rays of the rising sun emerge, the Romans can be seen climbing in long columns up the opposite hill. Then they go on to the slopes of the hill behind it, so that the first hill will serve as cover for the second. A camp, complete down to the last detail is pitched, with tents, stores and draft animals.

From the rampart surrounding the village, like a wall, arrows are fired on the enemy.

But, with utter unconcern, the Romans go about their tasks. Some of them lie down to rest; some continue to pitch tents, to tighten ropes, to pass around skin bottles, sacks, small casks, wooden boxes. The centurions walk about, armed, imposing, cool. The sun has not yet topped the range of hills. All around stand the Roman sentries, well-armed, scanning the horizon. The cooks have prepared great fires and are cooking. The Romans rest a while after their tiring journey, and sit down to eat their meal.

The Jews in the village are taken aback at the degree of composure of the enemy. At first, they think that as soon as the Romans reach the village, they will storm it immediately, and they are prepared for this. All the armed young men, and the old men too, and some of the women have not closed their eyes all night. And then the unexpected—the Romans are in no hurry. It is quite apparent that they have time. Whatever they do, they do without a trace of fear or anxiety. Just like fishermen, who, after they have carefully set their rods, do not worry further—so certain are they of their catch, if not tomorrow then the next day. It is as though the Romans think about the village people: Let the boys play a little.

Days pass. It is still as quiet as at the beginning. On the rampart, the scouts change and keep a sharp watch on what is happening outside. From time to time, people come up to ask: "Guard, what is going on? What is happening in the enemy's camp?"

Each night a few daring spirits steal out to hide among the rocks near the enemy camp. Their report is always the same—all quiet. Indeed, everyone who observes the enemy camp can see them busy eating and drinking, playing dice, laughing and jesting. The soldiers sit or lie stretched out, idly chatting. The captains too walk around unhurriedly, as though wars and battles do not exist.

On the fiftieth day after their arrival, about an hour after midnight, the order is given to take up arms and to storm the village. The soldiers, who have rested all those days, eaten well, and slept even better, are roused quietly, told to dress speedily, to arm and to form their ranks. Everything is done in the dark, without a rustle. Completely ready, they move at daybreak toward the village. Between the enemy and the village lies a deep valley, with a steep, rocky climb up to the ramparts. There is another way to the village, where the ascent is much gentler. Just opposite this point, however, at the top of another steep hill, there is a smaller village, also full of rebels. It suits the Romans to avoid proximity to this village, so that they will not be caught between the two fighting lines on the hills.

Before the scouts can inform the leader of the revolt, Yair the Reubenite, about the attack, the Romans have reached the valley and the vanguard is already scrambling up the paths among the rocks with catlike agility.

This is the crucial hour, as both sides know. If the villagers lose time, an hour, even half an hour, they will inevitably be defeated. Every moment is of fateful importance.

On the ramparts appear the first fighting squads of Yair, some with their faces still creased with sleep, their hair unkempt, their shoelaces loose. They look down at the men climbing up from below, and fury burns in their hearts. Arrows rain down on the Romans, but they crouch and take cover behind rocks, and continue their climb upward.

Here and there, someone topples over; someone groans, and rolls down, but those alive continue on their way up—not crowded together nor in formation, but singly, scattered left and right among the rocks, always climbing, climbing, up and up. Old men and women join the defenders, and roll down stones and great chunks of rock on the Romans. Women, with large cauldrons of boiling water, use copper scoops to fling the water down.

And still the Romans come higher and higher. Dozens fall, but hundreds still climb up. They come nearer and nearer to victory.

Suddenly there is a dramatic change. As the first rays of the sun strike across the heavens and herald the day, there is confusion on the steep slope. What has happened? Yehudah and his fifty men, who were scattered in their hiding places in the numerous caves, woods and forests in the area, and who have been spying on the enemy day and night, know by midnight that something is going on in the camp. It does not take long for them to realize that the attack is about to begin. They try to signal the village, but cannot because of the many Roman sentries stationed on the neighboring hills. As quickly as possible the news of the impending action is passed on to all Yehudah's men, together with the order to meet in the nearby wood. They fully realize the extent of the danger. So they attack the hundred men left behind in the Roman camp. Taken by surprise, these Romans offer little resistance. The partisans find great supplies, which they take as precious spoil.

Then they dart down the slope, overtaking and slaying from the rear the Romans still in the valley. They turn and run back up the same slope again, taking cover behind the trees here and there on the hillside. They begin to shoot arrows to the other slope where the enemy is an easy target. They can see the Romans clearly, even those hiding behind boulders, and it is easy to hit them.

Great is the consternation of the Romans who are low down on the slope, as the arrows take their toll. How could the enemy have reached the other slope? Those who are still not aware of the attack from the rear continue climbing, but others, among them army officers who find themselves caught in a rain of arrows from both sides, do not know where to turn. Meanwhile the shelter of night has vanished. Those up above the ramparts understand that Yehudah has stepped into the picture and new spirit enters into them. The Romans hesitate, confused. One Jewish squad comes charging down from the rampart and storms the enemy from above.

Had the Roman army chief known how few were those attacking from the rear, he certainly would have detailed a group of soldiers to attack them, and would have broken through, but since he does not know the truth and assumes it must be a large force, he decides there is no alternative but to escape from the trap in any way possible, to head for the top of one of the hills and to dig in there. Thus the Romans flee, with Yehudah's men and Yair's in hot pursuit. They scatter over the hills and the fields, and of the entire legion sent to punish the rebel village, only about two hundred men manage to return to the camp on Mount Carmel, by devious ways, all of them crushed and exhausted.

The name of Yehudah the Shibbolite is praised in all of

Galilee, the Emek, the Hills of Ephraim, and the Carmel. He becomes famous as one of the bravest Zealots. When he enters the village he has saved, at the head of his men, he is greeted with song and cheers. The girls of the village welcome him with drums and with dancing and singing in his honor, and in Yair's house a banquet is spread for Yehudah and his men, and, at the end of the repast, one of the respected elders speaks: "A people whose soul refuses to accept slavery is free; if its spirit does not enslave itself, no enemy can enslave it."

Yehudah, Avshalom and the others from Vale-of-Figs return to their birthplace to rest and to enjoy a few days with their families. Yehudah even brings a gift to the village, spoils of war—some camels, laden with bows, swords and spears. He divides them among the young men of the village, saying: "Guard this like the apple of your eye."

When Uziah, the Moderate, hears of the great quantity of weapons which Yehudah has distributed to the young men of the village, he is downcast and prophesies sadly to his followers:

"In the end, the Shibbolite will bring devastation down upon us with his actions."

6

Yehudah the Shibbolite gives up his stratagem of spying on the Romans as a peddler. From now on, he devotes his energies to a major new task—to form a complete legion of Zealots. One by one they gather around him—youths daring and brave, from the cities and villages conquered by the Romans. Soon they number more than a hundred. He takes care to arm them all with the very best of Roman arms. The group is divided into bands, which go into hiding in the mountains, forests and caves. One of his chief assistants is Yochanan.

The remainder of the original group, experienced in battle and maneuvers, head the bands. Yehudah's responsibility and work increase, and only at rare intervals is he seen in his home village. Suddenly, at midnight he knocks on the door of his house, and whispers, "Shulamit, Shulamit." His wife awakes, and, smiling, falls into his arms, kissing his hair, his eyes, and murmurs: "Oh, Yehudah, Yehudah, how I have waited for you . . ."

Before dawn, while the village is still wrapped in slumber, he gets up, embraces Shulamit warmly, kisses his son, girds on his sword and leaves the village secretly. Shulamit, clinging to him, pleads: "Yehudah, stay one day. You have enough loyal assistants on whom you can rely."

"No, my dear. I cannot remain. The enemy is becoming stronger every day, conquering and destroying. Evil tidings reach us from Jerusalem–famine, thirst, disease, civil strife. Men are crushing each other."

"Are you thinking of going to Jerusalem?"

"No, my place is here. The more we can undermine the enemy's power here, the weaker he'll be at the gates of Jerusalem."

One by one the young men are joining the legion. Not that there are many youths left, for Galilee is half destroyed, half deserted. Those who remain are in the throes of despair, since the last fortresses have been conquered, and since tens of thousands have been killed and slaughtered or sold as slaves by the Romans and by the men of Agrippa.

The whole of Galilee is in Roman hands. Samaria has been conquered. Jaffa and part of the region of Judah has been swallowed up, but Jerusalem still holds out on her hills, defended by the flower of the people. Even Vespasian, one of the greatest generals of Rome, cannot take Jerusalem. His armies are vast, numbering tens of thousands, their weapons are the best, the men practiced in war, but all to no avail. And as long as Jerusalem is in our hands, our sun has not set, thinks Yehudah. We still have hopes. The more the rebels harry the Roman armies in the other regions, the more they help Jerusalem and those defending her.

Then he hears that the village in the Mountains of Ephraim which he and his men saved from the enemy has suddenly been defeated. A large army encircled it completely, while a number of soldiers burst in from lanes and bypaths. The entire village was annihilated. The enemy left not one person alive.

This dark news depresses Yehudah bitterly. He says to himself, "If I and my hundred men had hurried there, the village would certainly have been saved from entire destruction." In deep sorrow, he sits for many hours, silent as a stone. The reflections which rise in him bring to the surface one word, as though crowned with gold, "Jerusalem. . . ." He thinks: "The body of the nation is ill, but if the heart is still beating, there is hope of deliverance . . . Jerusalem! . . ." His thoughts concentrate exclusively on what should be done: either to rise and rebel there, or go to Jerusalem. It is not easy for him to decide. He is a simple man, a villager far removed from the tumult of the city, and does not understand the spirit and customs of the capital. How can he choose the way of the Zealots?

But he smothers his doubts about himself, and assesses the situation of the nation and the country. The best of the forces in the north have been killed or sold into slavery; the major fortresses have been conquered; most of the villages have been laid waste and destroyed, and the few people that remain are in hiding for fear of Rome and her vengeance. How can he call for revolt? Who will join him? But if he and his hundred men decide to go to Jerusalem, of what use will they be there? What can a handful of men achieve?

Another course is to remain in the north, always on the alert; then he can use his forces to harry the enemy, to set stumbling blocks before them in every kind of way, uproot their forces, and meanwhile gradually assemble more men. As their numbers grow, so will his hopes be strengthened that they will eventually be successful.

He realizes at last that this way is probably the best. He forms his men into small bands, groups of three, groups of five. The bands are scattered among the hills, near the highways along which the Romans pass. Sometimes, they pass in large formations; at other times, however, small cohorts pass by, or ranks carrying provisions, or runners and messengers sent from camp to camp. Each time they pass, the bands of the Shibbolite storm them from ambush. Time and again, they annihilate the caravans, capture the provisions and arms, and store these in the caves.

This war from ambush is most harassing to the Romans. They cannot continue to send envoys, accompanied by three or four guards, but are forced to send larger groups. Yet even this method proves useless. For the men of the Shibbolite do not hesitate to storm groups of thirty, forty soldiers, even. The communications between the small bands of his men are constant and alive. They have special codes of signals: "Attack with a few men," "Storm with strong forces," "Beware," and so on.

Open warfare is difficult, but hidden warfare more difficult still. Open warfare takes place in open fields, whereas guerrilla warfare is in forests, woods, caves, hiding places, and the attacked do not know from where the enemy will spring next. Especially when the guerrilla fighters have someone to hide them in times of need, that is to say, the Jews living in the villages. The Roman army chiefs in Acre and Caesarea consult and confer often, until they evolve a plan on how to deal with it. They appoint some of Agrippa's men, Jews who are loyal to Rome, to serve as spies among the rebels. The Romans influence them with many fine promises. Not only will they receive monthly wages, but also a special bonus for each rebel captured. Not many weeks later, a cohort of Romans one hundred strong surrounds a cave near Yokneam and massacres seven of Yehudah's men.

From then on, special precautions are taken. Yehudah's men spend little time in the villages so as not to reveal their hiding places. But this does not help.

Soon the spies reveal to the Romans the identity of the leader. In every village they ask, "Where is Yehudah the Shibbolite?" Then they add: "To anyone who hands him over, alive or dead, there is a reward of a thousand pieces of silver!"

Although there are many money-grubbers, base traitors fascinated by silver, they do not catch Yehudah. On one occasion they nearly succeed. The spies discover and reveal to the Romans that Yehudah and ten of his men are camping in a thick wood near Charoshet Hagoyim. That evening, the small wood is encircled by hundreds of soldiers, like a chain tied around it, every ear pricked up to catch every sound.

By the light of the moon, about an hour before midnight, a Roman captain, tall and erect, whispers to a group of ten men who stand one beside the other: "Move silently behind me into the wood."

The ten Roman soldiers follow him. He takes them some distance into the wood until they reach the mouth of a cave. Here he orders in a whisper: "Draw your swords and enter. He is alone in the cave. Bind his hands and his feet. There is no danger."

The ten Romans enter the cave. The captain remains outside, gives his other men the signal, and they place large stones in the mouth of the cave.

The captain returns to the edge of the wood, whispers to ten more soldiers to follow him. They too obey. He leads them to the closed cave, and shows them a great heap of dry wood, and commands: "At midnight, roll away the stones. Place all this wood at the mouth of the cave and set it alight. See that no man comes out of the cave alive. Let them all roast inside."

The captain, none other than Yehudah the Shibbolite, returns to the edge of the wood with his men, who are also clad in Roman army uniforms, and they make their way through, and strike out on their own road.

Half an hour later, huge flames rise from within the wood. In the confusion, the Roman soldiers cannot tell who is who, and attack each other.

Yehudah and his men at that moment tramp as free men among the mountains of the Carmel range.

7

Beautiful little Vale-of-Figs, hidden away among the mountains, has not as yet come face to face with the Romans and is in a tumult each time rumors filter through of the brave exploits of Yehudah the Shibbolite. Some are proud of the hero, and some are angry and predict that because of him the whole village will suffer.

Of course, the Romans know of the existence of the village. The map of the Land of Israel is spread before them. But it is a small village, far from roads and tucked away in the recesses of the hills, so they leave it alone. When all the land is conquered, and the governor has to levy taxes, most certainly not even one tiny village will escape his eye. In war, however, things are less rigid, especially since all the villages in the area have been razed to the ground.

But when the Romans are told by the spies that Vale-of-Figs is the birthplace of the Shibbolite, they single it out for attention. First, with the greatest secrecy, they send in a spy to find out how frequently Yehudah comes to the village, what his activities are when he comes, how the inhabitants react to his being a rebel.

The spy, a Jew from the area of Acre, appears in the village as a peddler. He brings a donkey laden with all sorts of trinkets, cheap jewelry, colored scarves for the women, and so on. He stays in the village for a day and a half. Pretending to be an enemy of the Romans, he asks about Yehudah, whether he shows his face in the village, and so on. Not only Yehudah's wife Shulamit, but the rest of the village folk know that a spy net has been spread, and they guard their tongues. They suspect anyone who seems to be over-inquisitive, like the peddler. The village people do him no harm, but pretend to hate the Shibbolite, and say things which are the opposite of the truth. When the peddler reports to the Romans, he praises the village, and especially old Uziah, saying that they are loyal to the realm, that the Shibbolite is hated by them, and that they do not permit him to enter the village.

The Roman war chiefs consult about what they should do. Some advise, "Let us attack Vale-of-Figs suddenly, and take his wife and child captive. In the end, the Shibbolite will hand himself over of his own free will." Others argue, "No, we know from past experience that Jewish wives are courageous and prefer to die under torture rather than let their husbands surrender to the Romans. It is better to leave the village alone. When their fears have died down, Yehudah will return to spend some time at his home. Then we'll surround the village, and catch him alive and wipe out all his bands."

The latter suggestion seems preferable, so two spies are detailed to be "on guard," that is to say, to come to the village periodically and "see everything, hear everything and report everything."

A few weeks pass. The spies do their work conscientiously, but unsuccessfully. Yehudah is suspicious and decides to be extra careful. He does not enter the village except by the most tortuous paths, secretly, and at dead of night. He stays at home for a few hours and leaves by a secret path unseen. Uziah and the other village people suspect that the two men who turn up at the village from time to time are spies, but the word is passed around not to do them any harm. The spies exhaust themselves working, but come up with nothing worthwhile. Meanwhile Yehudah and his men do not cease their daring assaults on the Romans.

Eventually the Romans decide to adopt the first course suggested, that is, to attack Vale-of-Figs, and to take the family of the Shibbolite and others captive, as hostages.

Three days before they plan to carry out this attack, Yehudah learns about it and realizes what is in store for his wife and his son—torture, shame, slavery. He also knows what is in store for himself if he surrenders—death. And then what will be Shulamit's fate? He must get them out of the village. But where? What place is safe once the Romans are everywhere? What of Vale-of-Figs? If Shulamit and her son are to flee, the wrath of the Romans will be aroused and they will stamp out the village people in an hour. What then is the solution?

What if they should fortify themselves in Vale-of-Figs? The village is situated on a rocky cliff; the ascent is steep; the crops that year have been good and the food will last for many days. They even have a good supply of arms stored away in the cave near the village. All his bands could assemble in Vale-of-Figs and they are all courageous, strong soldiers. They know how to stand up to a large army of adversaries. In the meantime, perhaps salvation will come from Jerusalem? Not long since, secret information came through that Vespasian had returned to Rome, and the siege on Jerusalem had weakened. Maybe the report of salvation will come true, and in Galilee, too, the Roman hold will be weakened. Then the call to revolt will blazon forth and all the dormant forces will awaken, and rise to smash the yoke of Rome . . .

That very evening, information is passed from band to band to meet at an appointed place. Yehudah tells them there what the Romans are planning to do to his village, and he asks each one: "What do you think we should do?" One after the other, they answer: "Fortify ourselves in the village, and fight with everything we have." "Either way, our fate is death, or captivity, or slavery. Let us save what we can. Perhaps salvation will come from that. And these little sparks will blaze up into the flame of a great revolt, which will spread throughout Galilee and Judah."

The same night, they set out for Vale-of-Figs, and at dawn, they reach its vineyards. Yehudah orders his men to hide in the area. He himself, with a few men, enters the village. He sends an urgent message to Uziah and the other village elders: "In this hour of distress, let us take counsel together."

The people of the village gather in the tree-shaded open square in front of the synagogue. Yehudah tells them of the intention of the Romans, saying: "They are about to surround our village and to take the leading people as hostages. What do you think we should do? What is your ruling?"

They sit, terror and consternation on their faces and in their hearts. At first, there is silence. No one opens his mouth. Then Yehudah stands up, casts his eyes around all the faces, and says: "Brothers! We have three alternatives. You can hand me and the eleven youths who are sons of our village over to the Romans. In this way, you can make atonement to them. Or, I can take Shulamit and our son Gideon away from here, and the rest of the youths can take their relatives away also, and this may perhaps help in your subjection to the Romans, and they will not punish you. Or, we can fortify ourselves and fight to save our lives. The mountain is steep and high. We have abundant food. We have in the village one hundred men who can defend it and we have a great quantity of arms. We can stand like a wall. And if there is no traitor from within, the enemy will not defeat us. Maybe this revolt will spread from here and continue to spread all over."

Uziah's face turns first white and then red. His hands tremble. He gets up onto a stone, his voice shaking as he cries:

"My heart is not in rebels and rebellions. For look—all

our courage will not help us. We are as straws before the Romans. The way you are leading us, Yehudah, is the way of death. What will be the fate of the last remnant of Israel? Our Father in Heaven, have mercy on us, and may we return to be a nation among the nations!"

One of the farmers bursts out, agitated: "What do you mean, Uziah? That we hand over Yehudah and the other men to the Romans to punish, and that this should be their reward for their courage and devotion? This shall not be!"

"Let them leave the place, they and their relatives. Let them go wherever they like and we shall come before the Romans and explain to them as best we can that we did not act treacherously."

"And if the Romans decide to take vengeance on us and Yehudah and his men are not there to defend us—what then?"

Then Uziah calls out in a loud, hoarse voice: "We have seen these uprisings, like straw fires, flaring up in a second, and the next moment they have burned out; but between the flaring up and the dying out, they manage marvelously to achieve death and destruction."

"Death with courage is better than life in slavery," shouts one of Yehudah's men.

Yehudah gets to his feet and shouts impatiently: "What fate is in store for us? Fetters; the arena; our wives, concubines, slaves, maidservants. Look at the villages of Galilee. They are like one big fire. The flame of our soul is the flame of the Maccabees. Brothers, life or death?"

Uziah looks at the crowd and thinks, "The hand of Yehudah predominates. Most of them support him," and he tries to pluck a hidden string and make it vibrate. "If you want to sacrifice yourselves, do so. But the babies? These lambs, wherein have they sinned?"

Yehudah turns his head in the direction of the children. He sees Shulamit holding Gideon in her arms, and his glance is like a plea for her advice. Shulamit rises, trembling with emotion.

"Yehudah is right. We will not surrender. A life of freedom, or death."

She embraces her child, tears in her eyes, but she controls herself, and in a tremulous but clear, ringing voice, she says:

"We'll hide the babies in the big cave, concealed amongst the bushes on the hills opposite, until the wrath passes over. And the God of our Fathers will shield and protect them."

Yehudah jumps on a rock, his eyes gleaming, and in a loud powerful voice, he shouts:

"He who is for our country, come to me!"

The whole crowd comes to life. Together they shout: "Long live liberty!"

8

Only an hour has elapsed since the meeting ended, but the village has already taken on a different appearance. All regular work has ceased, and all hands are turned to defense.

Avshalom has been sent to give the word to Yehudah's hidden bands to enter the village. Very soon about one hundred strong tanned men appear. They join the village men, and together they heap stones on top of the rocks on the outskirts of the village to erect a kind of wall around it. Two village men are sent to the cave to extract the stored weapons, looted from the Romans. As they bring the arms into the village, these are piled up in one of the yards—a great mound of swords, spears, bows, shields. Then all men under the age of fifty are given arms for defense.

The women are busy with food supplies. They pick

grapes, mill wheat for flour, draw water. On the slope of the hill, down below the village, flows a spring. Cisterns have been dug in the village itself as well to catch rain-water, and they already contain a great quantity of water. Even if the village is besieged it will not be difficult to go the short distance to the spring to bring up water, especially as the path is completely hidden by the fig and other trees, and anyone walking along it cannot be seen. Nevertheless, the women are told to draw water, and to fill the cisterns and all other available vessels.

Thus the incessant work of preparation and defense goes on.

Meanwhile, the two men suspected of being spies appear in the village, the one as a peddler riding a donkey, and the other as a merchant selling cattle. They do not appear at the same time, of course, nor together. When they observe the busy preparations, they are most surprised, and ask very innocently what it is all about.

Then Yehudah calls them, and, in an authoritative voice, he denounces them: "Confess. You are spies!"

They turn pale. The peddler begins to stammer an explanation—that he is just a poor man, who earns his living by peddling. The cattle merchant, in a convincing way, says that he, too, is innocent and feels only hatred for the Romans. Yehudah flourishes his sword at them angrily, shouting, "I'll kill you, you traitors!"

At that, the false peddler takes fright, kneels and begins to plead:

"Forgive me, Yehudah. We have done wrong. We have sinned. But don't kill us!"

Yehudah scornfully pushes them with his feet, and orders one of his men, "Take them away."

When Avshalom comes home with his flock in the evening he can scarcely recognize the village. The men are working with tremendous energy. The women are bringing in water in brimming pitchers carried on their heads. Not-so-young farmers practice with sword and spear. The old women sit at the grinding stones, milling the flour, and even the children are engrossed with easier, but nevertheless important, tasks of different kinds.

Avshalom puts his flock into the pen, and runs to the rise at the top of the road, from where he can observe everyone and everything that is being done. He sees Yehudah next to the rampart that is rising higher and higher, showing the workers what to do. Avshalom goes up to him, and touches the edge of his cloak: "Yehudah," he says, "this time I will be among the fighters. I have been practicing with a sword!"

A smile flits across Yehudah's face. "Good boy," he says. "But Avshalom, I am afraid your place is with the children in the cave."

Avshalom's face clouds over. Sadly, his voice trembling, he pleads: "But I am big for my age. I want to fight with the men."

Yehudah puts his arm around him affectionately, and adds in a whisper, as if revealing to him his innermost thoughts and doubts: "Who can foretell what will happen in the end in this war? The future of our people lies in the hands of our children. You are the most intelligent amongst them. Your place is with them. This in itself is a very important part of the war."

These words, whispered in secret, in a tone of brotherhood, make a deep impression on Avshalom. Intuitively he accepts that it is his fate to remain with the other children.

The day turns to evening. Yehudah issues the order that they should rest for four hours. Later they rise to continue the preparations. Every moment is precious. He sends some men from among those raising the rampart to scout from the top of the mountain, and to keep an ear and an eye on the whole of the surrounding area.

The night passes in work and toil. The next morning, the women leave the village for the cave, clean it thoroughly, and spread straw on its floor. One of the village elders writes down a list of all the children of twelve years and under, who they are and how many. The scouts at the top of the hill report periodically what they see and hear. Their communications are reassuring. No Romans are visible. So the day passes in preparations. The ramparts rise and become like a high wall; the cisterns are full; enough flour is milled for several weeks.

About two hours before evening, the children are assembled to go to the cave. From all parts of the village they come, accompanied by their parents. Someone reads out the list to check whether everyone has come. Altogether there are fifty-nine. Only the infants in arms remain with their mothers in the village. The mothers carry woven baskets, which contain most of their food requirements. That morning they have made sure that there will be no shortage of water in the cave.

The sun approaches the top of the mountain in the west. It is but a bowshot from there to the tops of the trees at the hill summit.

The children, as children will be, are excited and mischievous. They love the whole affair. They see it as a kind of game—a cave, sleeping together, eating together, away from adults. They are the only ones who make merry at the parting ceremony. The parents, and especially the mothers, are pale and agitated, their hearts torn with sorrow and anxiety, their eyes full of grief, blinking to stop the tears that break through.

Tottering along, trembling and pale, old Uziah comes up. Leaning on his thick staff, he strokes his beard with his hand, and addresses the children.

"Dear children! The enemy is coming nearer. Danger hovers over our heads. Stay patiently in the cave, and pray to our God in Heaven to save us from the hands of the enemy. May brotherhood and peace dwell among you. The big ones must look after the little ones, with mercy and in brotherhood. The God of our Fathers will hearken to your prayers from the depths of the cave and will save us from ruin and destruction. Amen."

The women burst into weeping. They wail aloud, as though mourning a corpse laid out before them.

Yehudah arises, and, with a movement of his hand, hushes the crowd. Speaking in a loud voice, clear and strong, he turns first to the mothers: "This is not a time for weeping. We are removing our children from all danger, so that we can increase our power to defend ourselves. You, dear children, if you were big enough, I would have put you with the defenders of our beloved country, but as you are small and weak, we have to save you from harm. Now I command you not to leave the cave before we call you. Don't make a noise, and don't even sing. Talk softly to each other in whispers. Don't let anyone suspect that you are in the cave. For if, God forbid, you do raise such a suspicion you will bring great danger upon yourselves and upon us. My wife, Shulamit, will be with you. For the few days that you will be there, she will be a mother to all of you. You, Avshalom, the biggest of the children, you will help Shulamit with everything. Look after them. Not for nothing were you named Av-shalom, Father of Peace. Take care that there is peace among them, and may it be the will of our God in Heaven that when you reach our age the plowshare and not the sword will be your tool, with Israel dwelling in security in her land."

"Long live Israel!"

The tears stop flowing in the eyes of those crying. Their eyes light up and their trembling souls take courage.

The children set out. At their head walks Shulamit, erect and tall, her face telling of courage and understanding. Behind are the children, and on both sides of them, a procession of adults. Everyone is controlled and quiet. No one says a word. It is a great moment.

They reach the entrance to the village. The sun sinks among the branches of the treetops opposite, its rays still breaking through and spreading out over the western sky. In a couple of minutes, it will disappear. The procession stops. The adults turn back and only five people accompany the children. A few of the mothers complain at first, but everyone understands that there is no changing the order.

Shulamit and two of Yehudah's armed men march in front. After them, walking in single file along the narrow path, comes the whole crowd of children. Behind them, two of Yehudah's men close the procession.

Back in the village, the adults stand, rooted to the ground, pale, emotional, silent. Not a syllable. Not a whisper. The hour of parting is sacred and is not to be profaned by words. And then suddenly a little boy turns around and calls out tearfully: "Mommy!"

This single cry tears their hearts to shreds. It shocks all creation and everything in it. And the community of adults, which within a few hours will stand up to the enemy fearlessly, defying every danger, now bursts out weeping. Crying, sobbing, wailing. The mountain ranges seem to lower their heads. The sun hurriedly gathers in the last of its rays. Even Yehudah, so daring and tough, betrays his emotion. Down the hero's cheek the hot tears fall.

9

"If only the Romans delay forty-eight hours more, we will erect the rampart on the west as well. We are open to danger from that side now."

"It is true, Yehudah. On the west the slope is not steep. The vines and trees also hide anyone climbing up."

"We'll carry on tonight, heaving the stones and putting up the wall."

But the men are utterly exhausted, so much so that their fatigue may prevent them defending themselves if the Romans attack. Yehudah realizes the western rampart must wait. He appoints guards and orders the remainder of the men to lie down and sleep for a few hours.

Not half an hour after they are stretched out to rest, one of the scouts hears the footsteps of men marching from the northwest. He sounds the dreaded alarm.

When their two spies do not return, the Romans are not in the least disturbed. Assuming that there is some natural explanation, they still think it will be a simple matter to seize Shulamit and the boy, and a few of the relatives of the young Zealots. Therefore they do not consider it necessary to bother with a large army. They feel it is sufficient to send a punitive force to complete its task quickly and return at dawn. But, for safety's sake, fearing that Yehudah's bands may attack from the rear, they place one hundred and fifty more soldiers on the hill opposite, while the Commanding Officer, Julius, approaches with two hundred and fifty men as far as the foot of the mountain.

In the moonlight, Julius scans the high mountain and the paths leading upward, and gives the order to ascend at great speed. He is certain that after the defeat and destruction of the country's major fortresses, a small village will not dare even to throw a stone at a Roman soldier. He has barely given the order when the soldiers start climbing with astonishing agility.

Yehudah's men wake, seize their arms and rush to the rampart. The first of the Romans is already close to it. Yehudah, with a motion of his hand, signals to the men to crouch and to wait. Hearts beat like hammers. Only two minutes pass, but, to the defenders, those minutes are as long as years, as eternity.

The Romans note that no arrows are shot at them, no stones thrown. They conclude, "They're all fast asleep in the village." So saying, they cease to be careful. They stand upright and climb quickly and not in formation, as one would walk along a road where there is no danger. The ascent has tired them. Most of them are panting, sweating, stumbling, when suddenly—Yehudah gives orders to attack!

Most of the Romans are killed at once—among them Julius the Commander. One of the first to flee manages to convey the news of the defeat, of the great blow that the Romans have sustained, to the army on the other hill. The captain of the cohort is at first at a loss as to what to do, but soon pulls himself together, and dispatches a few of his men on horseback to the Roman camp on Mount Carmel, to request urgent help. He and the rest of his men come down to help in the difficult battle. But his aid is already of no avail. The high mountain is strewn with the slain. It is dark. From above arrows rain down. His cohort too is wounded. When the captain hears of the death of Julius, terror seizes him, and he orders his soldiers to retreat.

As for the defenders, victory uplifts their spirits and fills them with enthusiasm; even the Moderates rejoice. Only old Uziah is downcast, but he says nothing about his anxiety and his bitter doubts. For these are the thoughts that run through his mind: "Now, when the Romans overcome us, they will not leave one soul alive. They will wreck and destroy everything. And in the end the Romans must win, for this is the decree of the King of the Universe."

Yehudah, too, realizes that the Romans will certainly return with reinforcements to attack with increased strength. After the high spirits and rejoicing have subsided somewhat, Yehudah gives the order to continue the work on the rampart, with some of the people resting while others work.

Yehudah sends word of the victory to Shulamit and the children in the cave, and he also gives the order to take sweetmeats and urns of date juice to the cave, so that the children can eat, drink and be merry as well.

The work on the rampart proceeds slowly, for the people are weary. Some think: "The wall is only something extra. As fast as the Romans dare to climb up, we'll leap on them, and take them by storm, and that will be that." There are always those who prefer to boast of their bravery in war than to do any work. But Yehudah and the rest of the wiser souls in the village who realize the potential danger, call on everyone to work and work.

At three in the afternoon, a distraught runner rushes in from the lookout point at the top of the hill with the bad news. In the distance, dust can be seen rising high and thick; it is clear that a great army is moving along the road. Yehudah increases the shifts, spurs on the workers at the rampart. He hurries to the pinnacle of the mountain to see the approaching army for himself.

When he reaches the top, the army is not visible. Apparently it has entered the valley, and the mountains hide it from view. Half an hour later, the tail end of it can be seen on one of the slopes of the hills of the Carmel. The dust is rising high, like a heavy cloud in winter.

"A large army," reflects Yehudah. "The battle won't be easy. And," he conjectures, "their plan is to reach our village at sunset." He continues to reconnoiter, and then goes down to make sure himself that preparations are satisfactory. The work on the western rampart is in full swing.

The Romans do not hurry at all in order to arrive by

sunset. Some distance from Vale-of-Figs they stop to rest. They eat and drink. It is clear they think: "Why hurry? It will never be too late for this treacherous little village to learn its lesson."

About two hours after sunset, they approach one of the hills opposite the village, but they do not storm the village that night; they mount sentinels, and take note of all that is going on.

In the early morning, the villagers see that the Romans are fortifying themselves on the hill opposite them to the north. There is a valley below, and it is possible for people on top of one hill to carry on a conversation with those at the top of the other, if they raise their voices. The Romans begin to shower arrows on the village, and the villagers shoot back at them. Thus three hours pass. There are many wounded on both sides.

The scouts, guarding the village on the south, suddenly report a Roman phalanx advancing from the plain below. It has almost reached the foot of the hill on which the village is situated. This phalanx moves in a restrained manner as if preparing for the ascent.

The defenders divide. Some stay where they are and shoot from the north; others stand on the rampart and shoot from the south. The Romans do not even try to penetrate into the village. In this there is clearly a double purpose: to test the defenses, and to tire the defenders.

The attacking army is very large, so that some can rest and sleep, while others stand and shoot. Inside the village, however, the men are on guard without relief. They are compelled to divide the camp in order to man the ramparts on the north and the south. The other ramparts, too, need defenders. Even on the west, where the slopes are covered with vines and gardens, Yehudah places guards, not above, but below, in among the vineyards and the trees, so that if they observe anything, they can pass on the information to those above.

The shots of the Romans continue all day and night. Every now and then they begin a simulated attack, their chief intention obviously being to wear down the defenders.

Thus two days pass. At dawn on the third day, there are powerful attacks from two directions simultaneously. The defenders are very weary but they fight with courage. In reality, the Roman attacks are a feint; their strategy is to launch the real attack from the west, through the vineyards and gardens. From the early evening until midnight, they endeavor to ascend, with the defenders fighting fiercely to prevent them. At that very time, a small cohort breaks into one of the fig orchards and captures the paths leading upward. The scouts send up messenger after messenger, but each is killed. Meanwhile, these Roman cohorts penetrate deeper and deeper, hide and wait for reinforcements. By two o'clock after midnight, some hundreds of enemy soldiers are scattered in small groups throughout the gardens and vineyards on the slopes. They advance cautiously and surely upwards.

Yehudah becomes anxious when there are no dispatches for some hours from the scouts in the groves below. It is so very silent, so very calm. He sends two brave youths to find out the reason for the silence. They descend about two hundred steps from the western rampart, and suddenly are aware of movement in the trees. They crouch and listen, and at once realize the extent of the danger. The groves are full of Romans. They turn back quickly only to see the first band of five Romans climbing up ahead of them. Then begins fierce hand-to-hand fighting. One manages to get away, and as the village paths are so well known to him, he scrambles up very quickly and reports the danger. His comrade is cut to pieces.

Immediately, defenders are summoned to the western ramparts. The enemy is coming nearer, and has already reached the rampart. Suddenly desperate fighting starts. The defenders are so few, and the attackers are so numerous, about one to ten. Not only this, but the defenders are tired out from extreme exertion and sleepless nights.

Yet it is as though they have discovered hidden strength within themselves; they fight like lions. The women of the village pour vessels of boiling water down the ramparts onto the Romans, while others bring up new vessels, which they hand to those standing on the wall. Even the old men help. They pick up stones and throw them. The battle is desperate, terrible. The defenders kill and slay all around them, but they become fewer and fewer. All their strength and all their valor cannot withstand the disciplined soldiers of Rome. The legions form a moving wall of steel. Every breach is immediately closed up by other soldiers.

Suddenly a large cohort of Romans bursts through part of the rampart. Behind them climb cohort after cohort. They are winning. As day breaks, the enemy is right inside the village. The remaining defenders gather together from all the ramparts and form a square in the very heart of the village. On the ramparts surrounding them, Roman soldiers appear and begin to attack from all quarters. The valiant square shrinks, shrinks, shrinks.

There can be only one end. Almost all the brave young men are killed or wounded. The old men and women are bound in chains—slaves. . . . Only Yehudah and two of his men manage to break through the avenging swords and shut themselves inside one of the houses. Yehudah considers falling on his own sword to prevent his capture by the Romans, but instantly remembers the cave, Shulamit and the children. He says to himself, "It is my duty to save them." But hundreds of Romans surround the house, and break down the door. Yehudah and his two comrades dash among the attackers, felling men all around them. Then his two comrades are killed, and he is left all alone still fighting. His sword snaps. Hundreds of swords are brandished at him, but a captain shouts: "Take him alive! Chain him!"

Outside the house, the Romans destroy the village, robbing, looting everything in sight, seeking silver and gold, wrecking the houses, driving the herds out of the pens. The toil of generations is ravaged. Most of the people are corpses. The few that remain alive are fettered. Their tomorrow: shame, dispersion, exile to foreign lands . . . .

The sun rises on the village, once so beautiful, now a heap of rubble and utter desolation.

The Romans make their way down the hills, laden with spoil, their wretched captives shuffling along. Among them is Yehudah, both his hands and feet in chains. From a distance, he turns and looks with sorrow and despair at the village of his birth. An agonizing thought comes to his mind: "The children are still in the cave! What will become of them?" He turns back again, eyes downcast, and trudges on to meet his bitter destiny.

10

The cave of the children is to the east of the village, hidden behind a rocky hill.

Shulamit, Avshalom and the bigger children look after the little ones. They have food and water in plenty. The cave is wide and deep, and it is quite possible to keep the group comfortably in it. At first, they have difficulty in adjusting their eyes to the darkness, but after some time they grow accustomed to the pale, dim light that seeps through the opening, and lights up the entrance of the cave to some degree.

Shulamit plays with the children and tells them stories and legends. Whatever she has been told in her childhood she retells to them; and when the fount of stories from the days of her youth dries up, she makes up new stories about animals, kings and angels. Not only do her stories soothe and please the children, but she too, the narrator herself, forgets her great fears for her village and her people.

When the children lie down to sleep, however, and she stretches out on the straw, she strains her ears to listen to the muffled noises that reach them as if from under the ground. She trembles with fear. Depressing thoughts, fearful, terrifying, pass through her mind. All kinds of questions claw at her. What is going on in the village?

Many times she thinks of stealing out of the cave and getting closer to the village, but she is afraid of being seen by one of the Roman scouts and of drawing suspicion on the cave. On the third night, however, the last of the attack, she can restrain herself no longer. She creeps up to Avshalom and whispers to him that he should take charge until her return. Very carefully she crosses the rocks and draws near the village.

She approaches the village just as the Romans break in from all sides.

Tumult and confusion reign. Swords and spears clash. Between life and death, there is but an instant. The slain roll over; the wounded groan. Shulamit but glances at the dreadful sight and the thread of her life is snapped. Like the other slain, she lies silent, cold, stiff, saved from the fate of slavery.

All that night, Avshalom does not close his eyes. He is fearful and anxious about the fate of those in the village. Impatiently, he waits for Shulamit. Dawn breaks. Soon the sun will send a few pink rays into the cave, and still Shulamit has not come.

These are bitter and difficult hours for him and the other older children. The silence outside the cave is terrifying, as if every link with the world has been severed. In the gloom of the cave, an evil foreboding possesses them.

The oldest of the children meet together in the recesses of the cave, Avshalom, Rachel, Nafthali, Elchanan, Miriam and the others, and deliberate. What should they do? They decide that at twilight Avshalom should steal out, creep toward the village, and see for himself what is happening, and return immediately.

After they have made this decision, Rachel draws Avshalom into a corner and whispers softly to him, "Avshalom, I'm going with you." Dismayed, he says in a stern voice, half-scolding, half-loving: "It's very dangerous. You can't."

"If it's so dangerous, how can I let you go alone?" and two large tears roll down her cheeks.

"Rachel! Do understand. It's not for girls to put themselves in danger."

"If nothing happens, then it's all right. But if you come upon the enemy, even you won't win against them, and my fate is your fate."

"You must stay with the children and look after them. You cannot go."

As the sun sinks, Avshalom slips silently out of the cave and very carefully crawls on all fours from rock to rock, then stops a moment and listens attentively. All is deathly quiet. He crawls along again and listens once more. The silence surprises and alarms him. With heart thumping, and knees weak, he approaches the village. Another fifty steps and he will know. Suddenly his blood runs cold. He senses that someone is following him.

He bends down and hides behind a bush. Then he hears a trembling voice whispering, "Avshalom."

"Who is it?"

"It is I—Rachel. Forgive me." And in a second Rachel is beside him, shivering. In the oppressive silence, he can hear her heart beating. Avshalom takes hold of her hands in anger and in pity and whispers, "What have you done?"

"I could not stay. I stole out. Your fate is my fate."

Quietly they rise and move forward, he first and she behind him.

The moon is out, and after four days of living in the dark cave, its pale light seems to them like the noonday sun.

They reach the village. Before them unfolds horror upon horror, people lying slain, houses destroyed, everywhere the silence of death. From Rachel's very heart rises an anguished cry. In the quiet village where farmers once went their peaceful ways, the two children run distractedly from body to body, as they identify father, mother, brother. In their ruined homes they mourn their dead, shocking with their lamentations the mountains, the trees, the fields. The animals of the forests too are shocked. Their howling rivals the howling of the foxes and the jackals.

All of a sudden they see a tall figure. One of the Romans who has remained below with the village flocks in the valley, has heard the weeping and hastened to see what is happening. When the children see him they jump up, terrified. They are so frightened that they make no attempt to flee or to hide among the rocks. The Roman grabs Rachel with his hand, and laughing coarsely, cries, "You are my captive, pretty one."

When Avshalom sees this, he snatches up a stone and throws it with all his might at the soldier. But the latter moves his head to one side and the stone flies past. When Avshalom stoops to pick up another stone, the Roman draws his sword and strikes the boy a heavy blow with it.

His groans are muffled as he falls, rolling in his own blood. With a wild howl, Rachel leaps toward him, but the Roman seizes her a second time, saying, "A lovely little girl like you is worth not less than ten golden dinars in the market." He takes out a thin cord, ties her hands together, and drags her behind him as one may drag a calf to the slaughterhouse.

Rachel bites the rope with her teeth, but it is of no avail.

11

Avshalom lies as though his senses have left him. Only when the sun climbs higher and higher, and pokes its rays between his eyelashes does he revive. He remembers all he has seen the night before; he remembers Rachel, and his limbs seem to freeze. He tries to get up quickly but his strength fails him and he sinks down. He sits for a while, bereft of strength, depressed and despairing. The sun beats down from above, while dark thoughts, anguished and hopeless, assail him. There is no ray of light in all his grief.

Then he thinks of the cave, the other children, the babies. What can he do? With whom can he leave them? Who will look after them? Despair overwhelms him.

Slowly he stands up. His wound is not mortal. He walks a few paces, leans on a fence, turns around and walks back again. The corpses, the blood, the ruined houses, the silence of chaos and desolation, his fear for Rachel, all these things terrify him by turns. His heart is like a stone from the intense pain, and the fount of his tears has dried up.

Next to one of the houses, he sees an urn of water in the shade of the well. Who has drunk from it last? One of the people of the house or one of the Romans? Thirsty and weak, he gulps down the water. The drink restores his strength a little, and makes him feel better. He starts on his way, and climbs to the highest place in the village. From here, he scours the mountain ranges. Everything is steeped in the silence of desolation. He looks toward the northwest, and it is as though his eyes darken in their sockets. A little distance from the village, on one of the slopes, on the road leading to the Emek and from there to Acre, the Romans are driving the flocks of sheep and lambs, and among them he glimpses a yellow dress. Rachel!

In a flash, he runs full speed for ten steps, and falls. His strength leaves him. When he recovers consciousness a little later, he looks round with dark, gloomy, despairing eyes. Not a living thing can be seen. For a long time, he stares at the northwest point where he has last seen Rachel. His knees give way and he sits on the ground, wounded in body and soul. Tears stream from his eyes.

The sun reaches the top of the heavens. Avshalom rises and with faltering steps, like a weak, sick old man, he heads for the cave. The short trip drains his strength completely, and, when he gets close to the cave, he sits down on a rock. He gathers his scattered thoughts. What can he tell the children? One word from him will turn them into forsaken orphans, wretched little creatures whose today is bitter and whose tomorrow will be even more bitter. As he sits on the stone, thinking these sad thoughts, his friend Elchanan, a boy of his own age, peers out of the cave. He sees Avshalom, and runs out toward him. When he sees his face, he understands that some calamity has occurred.

"Avshalom . . ."

Avshalom puts his hand on his friend's shoulder, looks into the distance, and his look is dark. Grief and despair lie heavy in it. He whispers softly in a hoarse voice, bereft of tone, of life and freshness, "Elchanan, we are lost."

Elchanan does not answer. The two sit in dumb silence, the silence of helplessness. Avshalom pulls himself together and says: "Elchanan, Vale-of-Figs is as though it had never been. Everything is destroyed. There are dead in the streets. Not a man nor a women, not a sheep nor a goat, not a horse nor a fowl is left alive."

Elchanan sits pale, trembling, shocked. Then he asks quietly, "And Rachel?"

"Rachel was taken captive–from right in front of me, they took her."

And the fount of tears is opened, and Elchanan too breaks out weeping.

"Elchanan, we are not the only ones weeping. They are weeping in Galilee, in the Emek, in Judah, in the Shomron, in Jerusalem. Everywhere the sons of our people are pouring out their blood or their tears. We are the oldest of the children. We must guard the littles ones, look after them. If we are not for ourselves, whom have we?"

Elchanan answers, and his words are the words of despair:

"Why should we live? So that the Romans should steal us for their slave markets?"

As he speaks, he draws lines in the sand with his fingers, his face downcast. Both are silent, and at last Avshalom says:

"Listen, Elchanan. The corpses are lying around. We must not let the little children see them. The big ones among us must go and bury the dead and only afterwards will we take the little ones to the village."

"You are right, Avshalom."

"Another thing, Elchanan. I am injured, and need help."

With great concern, Elchanan asks:

"What happened?"

"The same Roman who took Rachel captive struck me with his sword."

"Why did you not tell me?"

"It is not a deadly wound. It will heal."

Elchanan hurries into the cave and a few minutes later the bigger children, Miriam, Nafthali, Dinah, David, Tamar, appear. Pale and tense, they stand before Avshalom.

Miriam goes up to him, takes his hand, feels his forehead, and says with great concern: "Avshalom, you have a high temperature. You are burning hot. We must bandage your head. You had better lie down in the shade and we'll give you a strong drink."

For the first time that day, a smile appears on Avshalom's pale face.

"Don't worry about me. I am all right. I have to be well."

The children lift him and with care move him under the tree near the cave. They lay him down on a mat and Elchanan says: "You, Miriam, look after Avshalom. Bandage him and give him wine to drink. He'll fall asleep, and it will be easier for him. You, Dinah, take care of the children in the cave. They may go outside for a while. I, Nafthali, Tamar, and two or three of the others will help to perform the last rites for the dead."

Sadly, the children go to perform the most terrible of all terrible tasks—to bury their parents, their brothers, their relatives and friends.

12

Avshalom falls into a deep sleep which lasts almost twenty-four hours, and when he wakes the next day it is nearly midday. The sleep and the rest have done their work and he feels better.

That night, some of the children sleep inside the cave, some outside. Dinah tells the little ones about the catastrophe, but in hints, in a roundabout way, disclosing a little and veiling the rest. The children nod off to sleep in their great unhappiness. About an hour after sunset Elchanan, Nafthali, Tamar, David and the others who have gone to bury the dead, return—depressed, withdrawn, silent. Their eyes are red from weeping, their faces drawn.

"Let us all go back to the village," Elchanan says on the following morning. This makes the little children very happy, since they do not comprehend the calamity that has come upon the village and their parents. Excited and happy, hopping and skipping along, they climb down the winding paths. When they reach the village, they scatter. Each one runs toward his home only to find it either destroyed or standing whole but empty. Not one finds his mother or his father. Only the young gravediggers know who has died, and who is missing, that is to say, who has been taken captive. Some stand in front of their houses, crying and sobbing; some sit as still as stones. The little ones sit very quietly until the sun goes down and twilight sets in. There is no mother to prepare their meal, to wash their bodies clean from dust and dirt, to put them to sleep, to sing them songs or tell them stories. Each one is alone with his mourning and his sorrow. Hungry, dirty, orphaned of both father and mother, orphaned of a people dwelling in safety in its land, orphaned of freedom and liberty.

The sun runs its course as usual. Whether it is a day of victory, whether there is mourning or joy, the sun comes up, shines and goes down. This has been its order and its habit since the six days of creation.

And so, even on the day after this night of sorrow and mourning, this night of whimpering and sobbing, the sun comes up again in all its glory. The children wake up. The bigger ones are quiet, angry; the little ones, when they remember, cry for their mothers.

Avshalom wakes and reflects; his parents were not found among the dead, so they must be captives. They are alive, but can such a life be considered living? His father, a quiet man, so respected by all, sold as a slave? . . . And his mother, so beautiful, so pliant, sold as a maidservant? He is shocked to the depth of his soul. Little Gideon, son of Yehudah the Shibbolite, a boy of three, sturdy and beautiful, comes to him. Avshalom remembers that Gideon's mother was found among the slain, and a heavy sigh escapes him. And Yehudah himself—was he really taken captive, and not killed? So perhaps . . . ? A ray of hope: maybe Yehudah managed to escape?

Gideon tugs at his sleeve and says: "I am hungry."

A sound of weeping can be heard coming nearer and nearer. Esther appears, a little girl of six, holding in her arms her tiny brother, a baby a year old. The baby is crying and the girl is weeping too, but as she cries, she tries to soothe her little brother.

Avshalom shakes off his despair, looks at Gideon, at the girl and her brother. It seems as if he has a vision of the future and all its terrors. He takes the baby from its sister's arms, quiets it, pats the little girl's hair, and holds Gideon's hand. He goes to the food cupboard, searching for something to eat. But finds nothing. In one of the corners down below are a few figs.

He collects them and divides them among the three children. The children chew the figs hungrily. Elchanan stands at the door and watches the little ones eating in silence. Suddenly there is a sound of quarreling outside. Avshalom and Elchanan go outside to see two children about eight years old with a loaf of bread. One is shouting, "I found it. It's mine." The other is saying, "It's all mine, I found it." A little girl comes along, puts out her hand, and cries, "I'm hungry too. Give me a piece of bread."

Avshalom goes to them, takes away the loaf of bread,

breaks it into pieces, and divides it among the children. The little ones are pacified. Each holds his piece of bread and eats it with relish. Avshalom turns to Elchanan, puts his hand on his shoulder and says:

"Please call all the children together at the open square at the well."

Elchanan climbs up on the fence of stones and announces in a loud voice:

"Children, go to the well."

He jumps off the fence, runs up the street, shouting:

"Children, all go to the well."

It does not take long. From all sides the children stream to the square at the well.

Their faces are sad and downcast. Where is the merriment and the naughtiness of the young? A boy of five holds his sister, aged two; two girls carry babies in their arms. All crowd together in the square. They wait. Avshalom appears. In his arms is a little boy. At his right hand is Gideon; Esther, the baby's sister, holds onto his left sleeve. A small girl bursts out crying; a little boy cries with her. Another moment, and they are all crying. One little girl shouts "Water." Another child joins in "I'm thirsty too."

Then Elchanan gets up and very quickly brings a bucket, lets it drop into the well, and draws up some water. The children crowd around, pushing each other, and drink thirstily. Then, pacified, they sit on the ground. Avshalom hands the baby to Miriam, gets up, and says:

"We are orphans. Our parents—a few of them have died and are no more; a few of them are captives in the enemy's hands. Everything around us is destroyed. It is hard and bitter for us. In a little while, we shall be without food, for the harvest has been looted. There are no clothes, and there are about sixty of us, mostly very small children. What shall we say and what shall we do? I have thought about this a great deal, and it seems to me that I have found the way for us. But we shall not be able to go along that way except by loving and helping each other. One for all, and all for one, in the end we'll achieve solace and happiness."

Avshalom's words rouse great enthusiasm, and as one person, they all rise spontaneously, and shout and exclaim.

Then Miriam says: "From now on, not mine and yours, but ours."

Elchanan adds: "We are all one. Together we shall work, and together we shall guard."

"You, Avshalom," says David, "will be the elder of the village. We'll listen to you, and do what you say."

Little Esther calls out: "You will be our Father."

Tears gather in all eyes. In a choking voice, Avshalom answers:

"I cannot carry this great burden alone. It is better that there should be three of us, Elchanan, Miriam and I."

"Three, three—the three-fold thread won't be easily snapped," somebody exclaims.

The children stand up and it is as though a spark of light is forced into the darkness of their hearts, so bitter and full of pain.

The bigger boys and girls disperse among the houses, and search and scour every nook and cranny for remnants of food, clothing and utensils. Underneath the great carob tree that stands on the high part of the street, near one of the houses that is whole, sit the three—Avshalom, Elchanan and Miriam. They receive everything the children bring, whether food or clothes or vessels. Soon a huge heap is piled up before them.

One child comes up, his face sad. "I searched in every house, in the stable, and in the yard, and I could not find one whole earthenware pot."

Another child, a girl, says: "I found a jar of olive oil in a corner of a yard covered with thistles, but I couldn't carry it because it is so heavy. I also found a linen dress of my mother's. Here it is."

Elchanan takes the dress and writes it down on the list, just as he has listed everything else. Avshalom tells one of those standing to go with the little girl and bring the jar of oil.

David comes along and says: "Part of our wheat was in a wooden barrel in the pit near the granary and all of it has remained."

Everyone is delighted.

"Good," says Avshalom. "Let it remain there for the present, but cover the pit very well."

"I didn't find anything," says one child, embarrassed and ashamed. "I looked and looked and there was nothing."

Avshalom pats his head and says: "Never mind. Don't worry."

Another says, "I found a silver coin under the bed. Take it."

And so each comes and brings the few things that have escaped notice. They stand around and watch. Then a sad thing happens. Dinah, who has ferreted and pried into every corner not only in her own house, but in other houses, carefully puts down a beautiful colored glass jug. Nafthali, who is watching like the others, leaps forward and cries:

"That's my jug. It's from our house. Why did you take it?"

Avshalom looks at him astonished.

"What is mine and what is yours—belongs to us all."

Nafthali becomes angry. "Who made you a judge and ruler over us?" he cries.

Avshalom conquers his sorrow and wrath, and says: "Take the jug and we shall not include you in the other things."

Nafthali takes the jug and two other things from the pile, and says haughtily: "These are also mine, from our house." He leaves the well, everyone staring at him with bitterness. He goes to sit by himself in his house, with the jug and the other things he has taken back, and thinks over what he has done. As he ruminates, he begins to feel regrets. He collects the articles he has taken, goes back to the carob, and places the jug and the rest of the things on the pile.

Ashamed and humiliated, he turns away, and stands behind all the children. Miriam gets up from her seat, goes to him, takes his hand and says: "You see, we are brothers and sisters now."

Not much remains after the destruction and looting by the Romans. Each one brings only a little food and various other things. Nevertheless, the piles grow higher and higher, and the things accumulate into possessions which can save the community from death and starvation for several months.

Thus passes the first day in the life of the assembly of children in Vale-of-Figs. That day and its events are to kindle many sparks of light in the hearts of the orphans.

PART TWO

THE COMMUNITY OF CHILDREN

13

A few months elapse. The end of summer comes. The children pick the fruits of the carob and fig trees. The work keeps them occupied, and gradually their peace of mind returns. They forget which is my vineyard and which is your vineyard. All the vineyards and gardens become the property of them all. All the harvest is collected and heaped up in one place. The fruit harvest that year is very small. Nevertheless this fruit is their staple food. The rest of the things they have found in the houses and in the storerooms are soon consumed.

The days of fruit picking should be days of eating one's fill. But after the carobs and ripe figs have been collected in one of the houses, it is clear that if they do not save, in the end they will starve.

During the rainy season, no fruits ripen. The grain harvest will only be ready in the spring. What will they eat?

So they divide the fruit into seven parts, one for one month, one for the next, and so on. This rationing limits each person's portion of carobs and figs. Hunger comes, and with it, much grumbling, and weakening of their strength.

Miriam, Dinah and Tamar stand and dole out the food to the children. They give each child five carobs and five figs. The children crowd around, full of complaints. One child cries: "And bread?" All the others shout after him, "And bread?"

Miriam, pale, pacifies them.

"The bread is finished, children. Eat what we have left. The days of winter will come. We shall sow and grow vegetables and have plenty to eat."

"But I'm still hungry," one child argues.

"Give me more carobs," begs a girl.

Miriam's eyes fill with tears. She caresses them, and says, "My dears, they are nearly finished too."

The child who has eaten his food looks hungrily at his sister chewing slowly as if saving the carobs from being eaten up. The girl, a year older than her brother, pities him and offers him her last carob. He puts it into his mouth and chews with zest. Another child standing nearby notices that there are still a few carobs in the barrel, and shouts lustily: "It's a lie. There are still lots of carobs. I'm hungry. Give us more."

Nafthali hears the child's complaint. He too becomes angry and argues: "I don't understand. Do you intend to keep us hungry? There are carobs. Let us eat our fill."

Miriam turns to Nafthali crossly. "You should know better, and understand what the little ones can't understand. Tomorrow is another day and we'll need food then too. Therefore, we have to give out the food we have little by little."

The children disperse sadly, depressed and hungry. Two little ones sit down to play. One says, "I could eat another twenty carobs and twenty figs."

The other replies: "And I could eat at least a hundred, and five loaves of bread too."

Even though the food is not enough to satisfy their hunger completely, the older children work unceasingly. There is so much to do: the rainy season is approaching; most of the houses are complete wrecks, and even the few in which they are living require repair; they have to prepare seed for the following year; they have nothing with which to plow; their worries are endless; there is a great deal of work, much more than children can cope with. The tiny children certainly cannot work. They play about, climb the trees. At times, they make a great find; at the top of a tree, a lone fig, a dried-up carob, which they thoroughly enjoy. The girls look after the small ones, wash them, comb their hair, change their clothes, prepare their food; and the big children do the hardest tasks.

One day, Elchanan and David are dragging stones from one of the ruined houses to repair another. Under the heap of stones Elchanan finds wheat in a small barrel. He cries out with joy:

"Look what I've found!"

Everyone comes running. The barrel of wheat can be

seen under the stones. The children remove the stones, throwing them here and there until the whole of the small barrel shows. Cries, shouts of joy!

"Wheat! Wheat! Wheat!"

"Today we'll eat bread!"

"Bread, bread, bread!"

Dinah pulls out the grindstones, spreads a sheet underneath. Nafthali brings her a milling stool. Dinah turns the stones and grinds. Everyone surrounds the miller and the grindstones, stares at the flour with joy and expectation. Miriam brings a copper vat, and prepares to knead the flour and bake the bread. Eyes sparkle with enjoyment. From all sides one hears:

"In a little while, we'll eat bread."

"Warm fresh bread."

"Will you cook white soup, Miriam?"

"Will you make matzot, too?"

Avshalom, who has heard from Elchanan about the wheat and has seen the small barrel, takes hold of Dinah's hands, stops the milling and exclaims:

"The wheat—we need it for sowing."

Dinah stops. Silence. All look with astonishment and despair at Avshalom. He is pale, upset but controlled. One of the bigger children asks:

"I'll ask you what my old father used to ask. If a man has a measure of wheat, should he plant it in the ground and die, or eat it and live?"

Avshalom answers:

"Yes, yes. That was what they asked in the days of the

prophet Joel, son of Ptuel, but what did the prophet answer? 'Even so, go out and plant.' "

The complaints stop and Avshalom continues hesitantly:

"We still have a few carobs, figs and olives. We'll be a bit hungry in the coming months, but if we plant this wheat, we'll have a harvest that will provide for us for the whole year. We'll eat and be satisfied; we'll eat and be satisfied."

Nafthali stops him with bitter scorn:

"We'll eat little by little and we'll die little by little. No, certainly not. We'll mill and we'll bake."

So saying, he seizes the handle of the grindstone and begins to mill. Avshalom stops him. Nafthali shouts:

"Children! Why are you silent? Don't you see that he wants to starve us?"

The children crowd together shouting:

"Grind! Grind!"

Nafthali's voice can be heard above them all:

"We're like his slaves. If he wants us to—we eat; if he wants—we go hungry. We'll mill and bake and eat."

Avashalom, Elchanan, Miriam, Dinah, Tamar, David stop them and will not permit them to grind. Some push—and some . . . shouts, noise, swearing. The grindstones are shoved out of position, the seeds scatter all over the ground. Nafthali gets more and more angry. His face is red with rage. He grabs a stick and strikes at Avshalom's head. Avshalom's face streams with blood. One little girl gazes at Avshalom's face and in a terrified voice, screams:

"Blood! Blood again!"

The word harrows the very heartstrings. Everyone falls back and stares with horror at Avshalom's face. Dinah wipes the blood with the edge of her dress. Miriam brings a cloth, dips it in water and puts it on the wound. Nafthali has also retreated, his face pale as lime, his stick still in his hand. He is excited and furious. Miriam takes the stick out of his hand and says with a sisterly rebuke: "What have you done? Are you not ashamed?"

Nafthali lowers his head and is silent. Miriam continues: "The small children cannot understand this, but you are already big. Don't you really understand that if there is no wheat for planting, we'll die of starvation?"

One of the boys, eight years old, nods his head and says:

"We'll die, we'll die . . ."

A little girl flings at him petulantly:

"Don't want to die!"

Silence. Nafthali raises his eyes. In a low voice, he says:

"But there's not even anything to sow with. Have we a horse or a camel?"

Elchanan steps forward and says:

"Now then, this is what Avshalom says. We'll scour the destroyed villages around us, and maybe we'll find some work animal."

Miriam raises her hands and hushes the audience.

"Very well—as you say," says Nafthali.

"Very well . . . very well . . ." Sounds of agreement are heard from all sides.

Avshalom sits on a stone and Miriam changes his bandage. David stoops and begins to collect the scattered grain.

A few other children bend down too and pick up the grains one by one and give them to David.

A child of five asks: "Can we make the flour back into grains?"

Everyone laughs. Some children shout: "No, no. How can it be possible?"

Little Esther remarks: "Perhaps we can cook some flour soup with the flour that has been ground?"

"Flour soup! Flour soup!"

Miriam gets up and says: "Very well, children. Today, we'll have flour soup."

So the children raise a cheer for her:

"Hurray, Miriam! Hurray! Soup! Today we'll eat soup!"

They jostle to see how Miriam collects the flour, puts it into a pot to cook the soup. That day the children eat not only carobs and figs for their meal, but they sip soup, hot, white, with olive oil.

"It's delicious," one of them says as he drinks the soup down with relish. "Next year, when we have a lot of wheat, we'll eat flour soup every day."

And another one smiles at him: "Even twice a day!"

14

The rainy days approach. Very soon it will be the planting season. The bigger boys like Avshalom, Elchanan, and Nafthali, although they are only twelve, know how to do all the work in the fields. At sowing time, they would often go to help their fathers with the work, and in the harvest season they would help also. Now they are prepared to sow, but what can they work, if all the living creatures have been pirated by the Romans? It is decided that two of them should make a tour of all the neighboring villages to see if they can perhaps find a camel or a horse or a donkey.

Avshalom and David set out on the search. They go to the right, and they go to the left, and continue thus for two days. They walk through virtual desert—not a settlement, not a herd, no living creature. Then suddenly in the distance they see what seems to be a settlement. Joyfully they head for the village, but are doomed to disappointment. It is not a village, but a heap of ruins. They begin to rummage in the broken houses and in the yards. They find skeltons of people lying exposed on the earth. They find many broken earthen vessels, broken glass, but not one complete object that can be used.

Then they see another village to the south, about an hour's walk away. Depressed and gloomy, they set out for that village, and it too is completely destroyed, except for three houses, which remain whole. In one house, they find some furniture, a broken sword, and a large earthen jar. In another house they find two skeletons of children, the walls defiled with their blood, a man's shoes lying about, and a torn silk scarf.

In the third house, as they open the door, they shrink back terrified. From one corner, comes a muffled heart-rending moaning. They stand rooted to the spot at the door of the house, pale, shocked, their legs paralyzed. Then Avshalom plucks up courage and asks in a strange voice: "Who is there?"

No answer. Avshalom raises his voice.

"Who is it?"

Something moves in the corner. Something is said in a whisper, but nothing can be heard. Avshalom takes a step forward, peering sharply into the corner. On a mattress, or rush mat, he discerns the figure of a human being. David too takes three steps forward, and both of them bend over and look. Avshalom asks again, "Who are you? Speak!"

The figure raises itself a little and the face shows. It is an old woman, wizened, her eyes sunken deep in their sockets. The skin of her face is of a yellow pallor. With difficulty, she lifts her hand and beckons to the young visitors. In broken language, she whispers a few disjointed words.

"Children . . . living . . . come . . . from where . . . water . . ."

Avshalom and David are horrified. It is as though death has taken all strength and understanding from the face of the old woman. Bewildered and full of secret dread, feeling weak and helpless, they stand beside her. In their short lives, they have already seen those slain by the sword, but before them now is life that is not life and not death—revolting. The old woman says no more, and closes her eyes. Suddenly her eyes, hiding deep within their two sockets, open. She looks at the two of them with a wondering glance, full of sorrow, and murmurs softly, "Water . . ."

"Avshalom, she is asking for water . . ."

"We'll go and look for some."

They rush out of the house and run all over the village looking for a well or a spring, and there, down on the slope to the left, is a well. With what can they draw water? They search and rummage in the yards and find a dried shell of a gourd lying about. Pleased with their find, they run to the well, and with a long stick they draw water up from the well. They are reminded of their own thirst and drink their fill of the cold clear water. Then they fill the gourd and run back to the old woman. The old woman is dozing and snoring. They touch her on the shoulders. She opens her eyes.

"Here is water. Drink."

She raises herself a little. With difficulty she holds the vessel of water in her hands and gulps greedily.

Avshalom begins to search the house, the corners, the storeroom, for a little food. He finds nothing. Out of his bag, he takes a soft ripe fig, divides it into two, and puts it straight into her mouth.

"Eat, granny, eat," he says, full of pity.

She chews the fig for a long time and with much effort. Her eyes open wider; she looks at the children and asks:

"Children . . . from where . . . ?"

"We are from Vale-of-Figs, the children of Vale-of-Figs."

"Vale-of-Figs . . . destroyed by Romans. . . . You. Where . . . ?"

Avshalom tells her what has happened at Vale-of-Figs and she says:

"So . . . so . . . children, orphans . . . no father . . . no mother . . ."

"What is the name of this village?"

"Gafna . . . the Romans . . . coming back from Jerusalem . . . killing and destruction . . . my son and my grandchildren . . . killed . . . my daughter-in-law . . . captive. . . . Woe is me . . ."

Her face twists. Her eyes all at once sink deeper into their sockets. Her mouth grows crooked and from between her lips breaks forth a stifled wail, thin, weak, frightening.

Avshalom hastens to give her more water, and pours some into her mouth without asking her.

She calms down somewhat, and makes a little motion asking for more water.

Not many seconds later, Avshalom asks:

"You said—Jerusalem. What have you heard about Jerusalem and its fate?"

The old woman raises her frail hand, and shakes her closed fist, her face contorted:

"The Temple . . . a mound of ashes . . . Jerusalem a heap of ruins . . . rivers of blood . . . the heroes captive. . . . We are lost, children . . . Our Father in Heaven . . . sin and its punishment . . . sin and its punishment . . ."

Her throat is choked, either by her tears or by her own words, and she is silenced. She closes her eyes and sinks into a deep sleep or a forgetting.

When Avshalom and David hear the tidings about the destruction of Jerusalem and the Temple, they sit in mourning on the earth. Avshalom, in a trembling, tearful voice, whispers to his companion: "The tombstone has closed over Jerusalem too, over the Temple. The Romans are destroying everything and we are in a desolate wilderness. Around us—darkness; before us—an abyss."

"Who knows if there are any settlements of living people left in our country," says David in dread.

"Jerusalem . . . the Temple . . . David, have you ever been to Jerusalem?"

"No, never."

"Nor I, but they say the Temple was the paragon of all beauty: Jerusalem, the most beautiful of cities. Prophets have prophesied on her every rock . . . the Holy City . . ."

Prostrate with suffering, the two living sit next to the half-dead woman, lamenting the destruction of Jerusalem, the destruction of the nation, their own destruction.

The old woman opens her eyes.

"Three days . . . without water . . . I got very weak . . . I was ill. . . . My end is coming near."

Avshalom feeds her another few drops of water. He comforts her: "You will not remain here alone. Come to us, with us. We will nurse you. You'll get better."

"No, no . . . my strength is at an end . . . another day or two and I'll be dead. . . . Children, don't go far . . . among the mountains opposite, there is a Roman outpost. They will catch you, God forbid, and you will be lost . . . slaves. . . . Woe is me . . ."

After these words, she lies still, looking at them, and gradually her eyes close and she falls asleep.

It is close to sunset. David turns to Avshalom:

"Should we return or should we stay?"

"We won't leave her alone. We'll sleep here. When she feels a little stronger, we'll take her with us. . . . Pity on her."

"As you say. We'll sleep here."

Until the sun sets, they go through the whole village once more, search and scrape everywhere, but find nothing. Of the provisions in their bags, nothing remains except a few carobs, a few figs. They sit down and eat, drink a little of the well water, stretch out in front of the door of the house and go to sleep.

In the morning, when they wake, they see that the old woman is still sunk in a torpor, her face strange, and her heavy snoring frightening. They go to the well, wash and bring water for the old woman. They sit beside her and stare at her strange face. For a long time, they sit there until the old woman wakes up, opens her eyes, looks at the children, as though she wants to make quite sure that it is they, and from her mouth issues fragments of speech:

"God in Heaven, forgive . . . take me to You . . . have pity on my grandchildren . . . have mercy, pardon everything. . . . The Temple will be built a third time. . . . Perform the last rites . . . grave . . ."

Suddenly she closes her eyes and a sort of rattling sigh escapes her, chilling the very marrow.

The children sit petrified, frozen. They do not know if they sit like that for a long time or short. In the end, they take courage, and Avshalom approaches the old woman and whispers to her:

"A little water, maybe?"

Then he sees that she has died.

The two sit beside her for a long time. At last, Avshalom gets up and says:

"David, we'll dig a grave and bury her."

Silent, the two go outside. They find no hoe, no spade, no pitchfork. They remember the half of a sword in the house nearby. One digs and the other takes the earth away in handfuls. At the depth of one cubit, they stop, because they simply cannot go any deeper. They return to the house, take hold of the dead old woman, carry her out and place her in the open pit. Then they cover her body with loose soil, find stones and place them on top of the loose mound. The heap of stones grows higher and higher. Finally Avshalom finds a soft smooth stone and scratches on it with the edge of the sword: "The last person left alive by the Romans in Gafna."

With deep sadness, they part from the grave, from the old woman, from the village. At the well, they wash their hands and faces, drink water, and even though they are hungry, they cannot taste anything. They go back in a northerly direction, for they want to reach the village they have seen in the distance.

The sun has traveled halfway across the sky. It is noon.

15

Half an hour away from the village, they meet an old man pasturing some cows and three skinny camels. The man is gray. His back is bent and his hands tremble. Avshalom and David come up, very pleased to see him.

"Peace be with you, grandfather."

"Blessed be those who come, children. From where are you, and where do you go?"

Avshalom relates all that has happened and concludes:

"But we have nothing to sow with—not a horse, nor a mule, nor a camel. Nothing."

The old man looks at the two young children. His pity is roused, and a tear runs down his cheek as he says:

"First of all, have something to eat. I have not much, but whatever there is, the three of us will eat. You must be tired from your journey."

"But you have provisions only for yourself. Why should you let yourself go hungry? We have some carobs and figs. We'll have enough to eat."

"Please do not be obstinate, my sons. Sit down."

He sits under the oak tree and invites them to sit down with him. Out of his bag he takes a little bread, honey, dates.

"Eat, children, eat."

The guests add their figs and carobs to the meal.

The old man glances at his two young visitors, shakes his head and begins:

"So you are from Vale-of-Figs. Thirty years ago, no, wait, thirty-seven years ago, I passed through your village. If my weak memory does not delude me, it was like a green-grass signature in the desert. Around it, rocky mountains, which could not grow fruit or flower. The village itself is on a sloping hillside and very lovely to look at. Already, many years ago, there were beautiful gardens of fruit trees there. Thirty-seven years! And now you say it is destroyed. This village too—alas! God has rejected us. They have burned the Temple. Jerusalem is laid waste."

The old man heaves a deep sigh.

"How did it happen at Vale-of-Figs?"

"Yehudah the Shibbolite would not surrender. He fortified the place. . . . The Romans . . ."

"Yehudah the Shibbolite? The hero—is he from your village?"

"Yes. The third house from ours. . . . He was a farmer before."

"Alas, alas, Yehudah the Shibbolite . . . a valiant hero

like him. They tell wonders about him. What was his end? He surely fell slain?"

"No. He was taken captive."

"Captive? . . . In the end he'll find his death in the arena . . . God on High . . . remember Your people, remember our fathers, our prophets. Yehudah the Shibbolite. . . . I am distressed for thee, my son . . ."

"Was your village destroyed too?"

"No. After the young Zealots joined the heroes of Galilee and fought at Gamla, only the Moderates were left and they surrendered to the Romans."

Avshalom longs to ask a question. At first he stammers, and finally manages to ask:

"And you, respected elder, were you too among the Moderates?"

The old man sighs and tears appear in his eyes.

"No, I was for the Zealots. My sons and grandsons were also Zealots. My grandsons joined the heroes of Galilee at the very beginning of the revolt and who knows what their end was, whether they are dead or taken captive. My two sons who refused to surrender, the Romans gave terrible punishment. They killed them, and took their wives, my daughters-in-law, into captivity. And so, in my old age, I have remained alone, lonely, without issue. Only one granddaughter of thirteen, who remained alive, have I to comfort me."

He concludes his words, his features contorted, and tears begin to flow uncontrolledly.

He is silent for a while and then adds:

"If only they had killed me instead of my sons, but they

left me alive really because all the heads of the village begged for my life. What will be our end?"

The cows have moved rather far away. The old man wants to get up and bring them back, but Avshalom stops him. He jumps up, quickly overtakes the cows, and brings them near the oak tree in the shade of which the three are sitting.

They are still sitting and conversing when a girl descends from the village. She comes up to the party and greets them:

"Shalom!"

"This is my grandchild, Bruria, my one solace."

"Grandfather, go home. I'll stay here. You can rest."

"You too sit down, Bruria. You think the calamity happened only to us. Look at these children. They were left as though in mid-ocean. The children of a whole village were left orphans. There isn't a single adult to look after them. How many did you say you number?"

"Fifty-nine boys and girls."

Bruria is moved. Tears shine in her eyes.

"Fifty-nine children and not one father and not one mother?"

"Not one. Most of them died. A few are in captivity. We are alone."

"And who looks after the little ones?" Bruria asks with deep pity in her eyes.

"The big ones look after the little ones."

"And who cares for the big ones?"

Avshalom smiles and says:

"We care for each other. We are one family. Since the

destruction 'mine' and 'yours' have been done away with. There is nothing but 'ours.' A few of us work at repairing the houses; a few look after the little ones. In the planting season, if only we can obtain a beast of work, we shall go out to sow, and the wheat will be ours—the family's."

Bruria's eyes sparkle, but at once a heavy shadow darkens them.

"You're together, looking after each other. And I . . ."

The old man sighs.

"My poor little Bruria. I am already old and feeble. All the work and the whole burden falls on her, the only one . . ."

There is a difficult silence, which Avshalom breaks with his question, "Can we obtain in your village a horse, or a mule, and a little barley for sowing?"

"Have you any money?"

Avshalom, his face red with confusion, stammers:

"We have no money . . . but we'll pay the debt from the granary and the vines next year."

The old man smiles.

"Innocent children. Who will believe you? The days are days of emergency. No man believes his friend."

He is silent for a moment and continues:

"Moreover, it would be better for you not to come to the village. A Roman captain and a few soldiers are stationed there—tax collectors. If they hear about you, it will be bad for you. It is better that they should not know that there is still someone alive in your village."

Bruria draws close to the old man and whispers in his

ear. The old man caresses her brown hair, and with a warm smile, says:

"You're right, Bruria. I thought so too."

He turns to his guests.

"As I said to you, it is better that you are not seen in villages which are still inhabited. The Romans will get to know about you, and you will bring great danger upon yourselves. To this very day, they remember Yehudah the Shibbolite with wrath. I am old and my end is near, and Bruria is alone. I'll set aside some of my property for you—a camel for plowing, a cow for milking, and a measure of barley. If God helps you and your harvest succeeds, you can return this to me if I am still alive. If I die, return my kindness to Bruria, for, besides me, she has no living relation. If God grants me life until next summer, I and my grandchild will come to you to see what you have done, and if I can be of help to you, I shall help."

Avshalom and David seize his two hands, so hairy and wrinkled, and begin to kiss the old man. Warm tears run down their cheeks, tears of happiness and gratitude.

"You have saved us! You are like an angel of God. May God bless you with long life, with good health of body and soul, and may everything you turn to, succeed."

The old man is moved by the warm words of his visitors. Bruria too is deeply moved.

Then says the old man:

"I saw our destruction and I said to myself: The end of our people has come. But today you have breathed a new spirit of life into me. You have told us of a community of children, of wretched orphans, forlorn, desolate, who want to thrust a plow into the field, to sow, to reap. You have told me of your life, the life of a family, without hatred, without jealousy. You have told me about children of ten who drag stones and mend houses and yards; your words are as oil in my bones. If we have a generation like you, my hope is still not lost. Not from outside will the redeemer come, for he is in you and those like you. If I am still privileged to see the fruit of your toil, I will go down to my grave in faith that the children of Abraham, Isaac and Jacob will not cease to be. Sevenfold will be God's anger against us. He will visit plague, war, exile, slavery upon us; the pride of the nation will fall slain; then, but a moment before complete extinction, He will have mercy on us, and permit new shoots to grow. From them, the nation of prophets will grow as a new plant. Happy are you, children, that you have restored to me the breath of my faith, my hope. So here is my small gift, and present my respects to those left of your families."

All the time, Bruria watches the two visitors with kindly warmth and friendship, and a bright, happy face. Her eyes express joy at all that her old grandfather has said.

"Now, Bruria," he continues, "ride home on the donkey, load up a measure of barley and come back here."

So Bruria jumps on the donkey and spurs it on into the village. Shortly afterwards she returns with the donkey staggering beneath his heavy load. Besides two small sacks of barley, she has brought other things, and even carries some herself. The old man stands up, and makes the camel kneel. He takes the things his granddaughter has brought

—the measure of barley, some broad beans for cooking, some lentils, a small parcel of salt, a jar of honey—and loads them on the camel.

"May you be blessed, Bruria, for the goodness of your heart," he says. He turns to the children and asks:

"Have you broad beans and lentils for cooking?"

"No."

"And honey?"

"No."

"What do you have?"

"Figs and carobs."

"Ah, then here is honey too, and broad beans and lentils and a little salt."

After they have loaded everything on the camel, the old man selects one of his cows that is with young, hands her over to the children, kisses them and says with warmth and emotion:

"God will help you. Continue as you're doing, and you will succeed. I see in you that you will raise a generation pure of heart, with clean hands, doing loving and good deeds."

Avshalom and David thank the old man and his granddaughter. Tears of joy dance in their eyes, and so they depart, one leading the camel and the other stepping out behind the cow.

16

The days of winter in Vale-of-Figs are filled with activity and interest, also with sufferings and sadness.

In the month of Kislev, good rains fall. The earth is saturated with water and becomes green with young shoots. The sun comes out and the soil dries, making it possible to plow and sow. Since they have but little seed, only a small area in the valley is leveled for wheat, and a small area on the slope for barley. The day that they go down to sow is like a holiday in the little village. On the camel, they load a small sack of barley and the wooden plow. Nafthali leads the camel and all the children of the large family stream behind him. Even the little ones trail behind the crowd, and when they reach the field which has been leveled for the sowing of the barley, Nafthali stops, makes the camel kneel, unloads the barley and the plow. Avshalom is wearing a plowing-apron; he puts a few grains in it and begins to step out and sow. Nafthali harnesses the camel and thrusts the plow into the ground. A furrow opens. One person plows and the other sows, while all the children stand around, walk here and there and jump on the rocks, their faces shining with joy.

"They're planting barley," whispers a little girl.

"They'll sow wheat also," adds another child.

"We won't be hungry for bread or soup or gruel."

"We'll have everything."

"When will the barley sprout?" asks one little child.

"In a few days."

"And when will there be ears of corn? When will there be barley seed?"

"Only in the spring."

"Only in the spring?"

Gideon, son of Yehudah the Shibbolite, goes up to Avshalom, tugs at the apron, and begs:

"Avshalom, let me sow a little too."

Avshalom gives him a handful of barley, shows him how to sow, and Gideon scatters the grains in the earth. He runs across the field boisterously, shrieking, "I sowed too!"

Another child goes to Nafthali and pleads, "Let me plow a little."

Nafthali answers with a smile: "All right. The two of us will plow. Both you and I will hold the plow."

The child holds the handle of the plow, walks beside Nafthali and asks him: "Will we always have only one plow?"

"No. If we obtain another horse or camel, we'll plow with the two plows the Romans left us."

"When I'm big, I'll plow by myself, won't I?"

"Of course."

So happy are the children that day that they forget all about food and drink. The planting continues for some days and the day after it is completed, the skies darken with clouds. The rains come down and stop; come down again and stop; and come down. Eventually the heavens clear, and become bright and limpid, without even a cloud as big as a fist. The sun warms the earth, making it bright and dry.

After a few days, Elchanan goes down to the valley to see if it is in fit condition for plowing. He is thrilled to find that the barley is sprouting all over, as if a soft silky green carpet has been spread. He rushes back to announce the good news, and while he is still talking, everyone runs down to see, and they stand all around the field, overjoyed —the barley has sent up shoots!

The next day they begin sowing the wheat and again everyone is in the valley celebrating happily, shouting, making merry. It seems as if the valley itself, which only a few months before was stained with blood, and witnessed the terrible spectacle of murder, is rejoicing in the laughter and mischief of the children. When they have finished sowing the wheat, they plan to hoe and weed the vineyard and the fruit trees, a great deal of very tiring work. Morning after morning, they get up early, and, hoes on their shoulders, go down to the vineyards and the orchards, and hoe faithfully and devotedly. As they busy themselves with these many and varied tasks, the village slowly returns to its former beauty, with the vines and trees in blossom and the mountains covered with green. In the wheat and barley fields, the crop is growing taller. Plants, trees, vegetables, drawing sustenance from the depths of the earth, soaking in the rays of the sun, cover themselves as though they are saying, "What have we to do with hatred between human beings? What have we to do with war of man against man? We are plants that grow."

The days are bright and beautiful, neither warm nor cold; the countryside is glorious. The work is pleasant and stimulating. Without, it is a world of magic and quiet, but within, in the secret recesses of the heart, mourning and sorrow still lie heavily.

In the winter months, the scarcity of food becomes more severe. The broad beans and lentils have been eaten; the honey is finished; more figs have been eaten than the monthly ration; as usual, the desire to eat more becomes stronger in the winter, especially when there is more work. So there are not only pleasant hours but also hours of complaint, weeping and reproach.

At times a child takes half a carob or a fig away, and a quarrel breaks out, followed by discussions and arbitrations, with each side shouting, "I am right."

In addition to these small tribulations, comes a great sorrow. During the heavy rains at the end of Tevet, Nahum, a child of two, is taken ill with a sore throat, high temperature and choking. The children stand around him, not knowing what to do. Some try to remember what their mothers used to do when they were ill, what treatment they were given. They remember that their mothers heated certain herbs and put them on the throat, and boiled other grasses and gave them the liquid to drink.

They try with the grasses but do not succeed. The child looks worse, his temperature rises, and he writhes in pain and suffering. Only a few of them go out to work for the rest are busy with the sick child. They take turns sitting at his side, giving him spoonfuls of water, changing his bandages, and sharing his suffering. The next day he is worse; he refuses to permit anything to pass his lips, he moans and tosses and turns ceaselessly. The older children go around at a loss, and the little ones are depressed. They do not laugh, or get into mischief. The illness drags on for some days, and then the child gives up his soul to God.

Who can describe the great mourning in this family, the family of children? Their calamity has united them as brothers and sisters in living and caring for one another. And now one of them has been torn from their midst. Nahum, so little and so lovable, who has only just learned to speak, has been taken away. Days pass before lightheartedness returns, until they can accept the tragedy. Even when laughter is once more heard, every now and then they mention their brother Nahum and his bitter fate.

In the middle of Shvat, a bad accident befalls them. Little Esther climbs one of the trees, falls and breaks her arm. Another child, who is playing with her, runs to tell Miriam what has happened. Everyone who hears the bad news is frightened and hurries to the orchard. They find Esther lying on the ground moaning and groaning. The children lift her and carry her to her house but do not know what to do to help her. There is no physician to help them, not even one grown-up who knows something about such matters.

Miriam quickly begins to apply cold water compresses on the arm, because she remembers that the first thing you do is to apply water compresses. But what next? The bigger children are summoned from the vineyard and they too stand and watch her in her agony and do not know how to save her.

Then all at once, Nafthali says to Avshalom: "When I was little, I once saw how they bandaged the broken leg of Reuben, our neighbor. A woman from one of the nearby villages put the leg between long sticks, tied them on tightly with a long thin rope and ordered Reuben, 'Lie still and don't move your leg.' He lay there for I think three weeks. Maybe we should try to do the same?"

The children hear his words and begin to vie with each other. One says, "It is very dangerous and we won't do it in case we do some damage." Another says, "If we do nothing, that is certainly very dangerous too." Only two hours later, when Esther is still crying bitterly from her terrible pain, does Nafthali come back from the orchard where he has selected straight thin branches and removed the bark from them carefully; he has taken a thin, long rope and patiently unraveled all the knots; then he has folded up the rope, some cloth, a strip of old dress, and placed the whole bundle in a corner. He goes to Esther, sits down beside her, carefully takes her broken arm and examines it. "There are no signs of blood, that is to say, the bone is broken inside." He strokes Esther's hair and asks her:

"Esther, should I bandage your arm? Or are you afraid I'll increase your pain?"

"Do what you like, for there is no pain like my pain."

When the children hear what she says, they give up their opposition and say to Nafthali:

"Maybe, in spite of everything, it will help. It is better to try."

Nafthali gets his bundle from the corner. He sends all the smaller children out of the room, and only the bigger ones remain to help. The big ones hold Esther, and Nafthali covers her arm with the soft cloth and binds it firmly, and afterwards places it between the sticks. A few of these are not suitable, and he shortens them a little. Miriam holds the sticks to prevent them from spreading and Nafthali ties the rope around and around closely, until the sticks are not visible. At the end, he ties a last tight knot, makes Esther lie on the side of the good arm and says:

"Esther, you must lie either on your back or on your other arm, so as not to hurt the broken arm. And don't move it at all. Now, you had better try to go to sleep."

All the time that Nafthali has been busy tying the rope tight, Esther has moaned with pain, but when he has finished his work, it seems to her that she feels somewhat better. Miriam gives her a hot drink and an extra fig more than the ration, and she falls asleep.

The next day, she gets up, her arms supported in the sling bound to her neck. After a month, the splints are removed and her arm is sound and healthy.

Never did anyone celebrate and rejoice as does Nafthali. Everyone congratulates him and praises him to the skies.

Then another illness attacks seven of the children. The sufferers have a heavy dry cough, and their temperatures rise. They become very hoarse and lose all appetite for food. The illness is not severe and not dangerous, but the sick children become thinner and thinner and writhe in pain, choking, when the coughing seizes them. They are weak and pale; all merriment deserts them, and they lie sad and inert, as if they are not interested in anything in the world.

Miriam says: "Let us put the sick children in one room and it will be easier to look after them."

They do this. And indeed, it is easier to care for them, but still the children do not mend. Sadness rules in all the small camp; singing and joking stop, and all eyes are drawn to this room, the sickroom.

One fine morning Elchanan rushes in from one of the yards, runs from house to house and from room to room, shouting the news:

"The cow has had a calf! The cow has had a calf!"

Half naked, the children, big and small, run out into the yard where the cow has given birth. There before them is the little calf, reddish, frisky and full of life, jumping about in the yard and onto the children as if to say, "Let us be friends and play together."

That day the children forget Esther and her hand; forget the seven sick children lying in their room and their coughing that can be heard a long way off. Enthusiasm comes into the heart of the camp as everyone stands around the calf, smoothing her soft coat, looking into her eyes and giving her greens to eat—although she still cannot chew and only smells them with her nostrils.

It is little Gideon who first breaks the news to the sick children.

"A calf has been born—a red one, lovely, jolly, naughty. It'll be our sister."

The eyes of the sick change. They shine with happiness. The weakness seems to vanish all at once. They all get up and want to run off to see the calf.

Tamar comes in shouting, "Children, where are you going?"

"A little calf has been born!" they burst out together. "We want to go to see it."

"Impossible, children, you are sick with temperatures, and weak."

The patients will not give up their desire to see the calf. Tamar says:

"You know what? We'll bring the calf here!"

"Oh, yes!"

"Hooray!"

"Bring the calf here!"

Tamar goes off. A little later, a great procession comes along, and in the middle of it is the calf. Shouts of joy and merriment! They come to the door of the sickroom, push the calf inside. She stands there for a moment, looks around her and as though surprised at what her eyes see, lets out a "Moo-oo" and jumps from child to child. The patients forget that they are sick, forget their coughs, their pains. With excitement and happiness they stroke her, feel her ears, kiss her forehead.

That day there is a feast in Vale-of-Figs. Joy is added to joy. Milk! Milk! It is true for the first three days they cannot bear the taste of the milk, but the fourth day the milk is already sweet and its taste good. The milk is brought to the sickroom, and given to the patients, and this it is that helps their cough, until eventually they recover completely.

17

Spring. The season of the barley harvest. All members of the children's community are in the barley field, near the valley. The reapers are bathed in sweat. They stand crowded together, with joy written all over their faces. A year ago, too, and for years and years before that, reapers have stood in these fields, and reaped. Then, too, the reapers were tired out, sweating, their faces streaming with happiness and joy, but a year ago and for years and years before that the reapers were spread out through the expanse of the fields, each man on his own plot. Now all of them are on one small plot as one family. Then big people reaped, and now there is not a single adult to be seen. Only last year under the lone oak there were cradles, and inside them babies. The mothers, when they stopped work, would go to them and feed the babies at the breast. Now there is not even one cradle, no old people, no adults, and no babies.

It is a world of children. The big children reap, and even the little ones are busy—they plait wreaths out of straw or the ears of grain, glean the leavings after the reapers, run and bring water from the spring to break the thirst of the reapers. Avshalom is thinking: "The barley will be sufficient for the whole year for food and for seed. The wheat too . . . it looks as if the harvest is good. It will be enough for bread and for seed. The vines as well . . . there are good signs . . . the grapes will be plentiful . . . we'll eat and be satisfied. We will dry some raisins. The figs too and the carobs are abundant, and the olives are by no means few." He sums up, to himself: "Not bad. We won't starve yet. The little ones will have enough to eat and will get well and strong." He is still thinking pleasant thoughts, when a shadow crosses his face. "From what will we deduct in order to repay the old man the price of the camel, the cow and the barley? We need the wheat and the barley. There will be an excess of grapes, but how can we transport them in order to sell them, and where to? Maybe we can sell a few olives? If we sell the surplus, we need at least one more horse so that we can sow more."

The hour of noon approaches. Except for dry carobs, some figs and a dish of cooked grass roots, what had they eaten that day? Hunger has already been gnawing for the past hour. Soon it will be lunch time, but what will they eat? Once again the same old foods which cannot satisfy. And then Miriam appears at the top of the mountain, seeming to glide along the winding path. In her hands she is holding a vessel, and on her head a large bundle wrapped in a cloth. Behind her trail two children, who also have bundles in their hands.

"Miriam is coming. Soon we'll eat the midday meal."

"I am as hungry as three hungry men."

"And I have been hungry since this morning. I am tired of carobs. I cannot look at them."

"But we won't be hungry forever . . . soon . . ."

Miriam comes up to a fig tree with broad spreading branches and puts down her bundles. The children accompanying her lay theirs down too, and come running down to the reapers, calling:

"Come to eat! To eat!"

The reapers put down their scythes; the sheaf-binders their sheaves; the little children leave their games, and everyone heads for the fig tree, for the meal.

"Look! Bread. Bread."

"Fresh warm bread!"

"Miriam, from where?"

"I threshed a little barley. I milled it and baked it."

"The first day of bread. The first piece!"

They fall upon the bread as though in the grip of starvation, but Miriam scolds them lovingly:

"There is enough bread for everyone. Sit down nicely. Don't snatch. Eat and relax."

Everyone sits, some near the tree trunk, some under the branches that reach down and touch the ground, and those that can find no shade sit in the sun.

Miriam pours hot white soup from the big pot into the large earthenware bowls.

"Oh! Milk soup and barley grits. Lovely!"

"When did you manage to do all this?"

"I wanted you to have a good feast on Harvest Day. The day before yesterday I gathered the ears, threshed, and prepared the grits."

The children grab hold of the wooden spoons, seize the bread and eat with relish.

"This is really a feast!"

"A royal feast!"

"I could eat soup like this every day!"

A small child who sits next to Miriam looks at her and asks quietly: "Will we eat soup like this tomorrow also, Miriam?"

"Tomorrow also, dear."

For the first time since the bread was finished, the family sits and eats a fully satisfying meal. Afterwards, they stretch out on the ground to rest, and little Esther, whose voice is sweet and pleasant, begins to sing the song of the reapers.

After singing and resting, they go back to reap. The sun inclines westward. A cool refreshing wind blows gently. The reapers work with additional energy. Some reap, others bind sheaves, and the little ones make themselves crowns of ears of corn for their heads. Indeed, the old shepherd is right. Jerusalem is in ruins, the Temple lies in ashes, the Sons of Zion and her Daughters are being sold in the markets of the world as slaves and maidservants, but if, in one little corner, in the valley of Vale-of-Figs, a generation of young people is reaping and singing the reapers' song—the flame has not been extinguished. The sparks will ignite; the flames of life will burst forth, and the nation will surely arise reborn.

18

In the summer months, supplies are abundant and pour in as though from all quarters. Bread is given out in sufficient quantities and there are no longer quarrels over a small slice. There are also grits from which porridges and soups are cooked. Then the grape season comes, red grapes, juicy, sweet, fragrant. Before daybreak, the little covey of children disperses among the vines, and while the grapes are still chilled from the cold of night, and wet as though washed in the morning dew, they harvest the grapes, bunch by bunch, and at the same time, fill their stomachs. Tamar remembers how her mother used to bake all sorts of cakes with flour and grapes; and for the first time, she tries to do as her mother did. After baking, however, there is more raw dough than baked. This is only at first. The more she bakes, the more she improves, and in the end the cakes are excellent and please both the little ones and the older children.

One day Avshalom walks through the vineyards, comes home and remarks: "This year there are so many grapes, now all ripe. Let us make a little wine, although most of the grapes we'll dry as raisins."

The tiny children raise a cry of joy:

"Raisins! Raisins!"

"Miriam, do you know how to cook gruel from groats and raisins?"

"And cake with raisins? How lovely!"

"Right now I could eat raisins. I'm tired of grapes!"

Avshalom adds:

"We won't keep all the raisins for ourselves. We have to pay off our debt for the camel, the cow and the barley. We'll pay partly with raisins, partly with oil, and partly with carobs."

Nafthali, who has changed in outlook and now understands generally that there is no such thing as "mine" and "yours" but only "ours," still loves stuffing himself with food, and always imagines that he is given less than the others. Now, when he hears Avshalom's proposal, he says:

"If we give away part of our raisins and our oil and our carobs, what will we eat in the winter? Won't we be facing hunger again?"

One of the little children, hearing this, declares:

"I don't want to go hungry again."

"What? Will we be hungry again?" demands a little child of four.

Avshalom stands up and explains:

"You are becoming angry for nothing. Who wants to go back to the days of hunger? We shall not sell the wheat and the barley, but we can sell fruit. We'll sit down and calculate how much fruit we need for ourselves for the whole year, and the rest we'll sell and pay off our debt. Remember, a debt is holy. Let us not forget that the old man saved us at a time of great danger, saved us from perishing."

But Nafthali persists:

"And again we'll eat figs and carobs, each one just so many, weighted and counted?"

"No. Everyone may eat his fill. We won't be strict. But even after we've eaten as much as we like, there will still be fruit left over."

These words put Nafthali at ease and he is silent.

The days are crowded with work in the vineyards—picking the grapes, transferring them to the village, spreading them out on the flat roofs to dry as raisins. Even children of six help in the work. After the grapes will come the fig season. These too they will pick and dry. Each task has its season.

In the vineyards, the harvesters work between the branches. The sun burns down from above, and the sweat pours down their faces. The work with figs is quite different. The children climb on the trees, sit or stand on the branches, and so, deep in the shade, they harvest in woven baskets. The smaller children work above, the bigger ones below. They can reach the branches near the ground, and with a special kind of stick gather the fruit in baskets. At times, they bend a branch downward, and as they work, pop a ripe fig, big and juicy, into their mouths.

There are also happy interludes. Little Esther, her hand now healed, is sitting on a branch, energetically picking the figs and putting them in her basket. She begins to sing. Her voice is soft, clear and pleasant. The crowd of harvesters hidden among the big thick trees listens in silence to her song. Then individual voices burst forth from among the branches, and soon all the children are caught up in song, exactly like the birds of Galilee that abound in huge numbers, and hop from branch to branch, and pour their hearts out in song. Just so it is with this choir of harvesters, tucked away among the foliage. Since the children are invisible, it seems as though the very garden itself is singing.

One day, something happens which at first upsets them and then makes them very happy. Because of it, there is a half-holiday. While working in the fig orchard, one of the children at the edge of the garden looks up and sees a man riding on an ass. He is coming down the path between the tracks on the hill opposite, heading straight for the village. The child who sees the rider slips down the tree and, frightened and appalled, runs by a secret trail through the trees to report to Avshalom: "A man on an ass is riding toward us."

All the children are alarmed, Avshalom too. Who knows who the visitor may be? Maybe a messenger from the Romans? He tries to stop the children from coming down from the trees, but is too late. They all jump down, put down their baskets, and run to the edge of the orchard to see the visitor.

When they reach the end of the garden, there is no rider to be seen, for the path twists among the rocks and hides him. The children huddle together, their eyes strained wide, their hearts beating, awaiting the visitor, who will soon reappear to the right of the rocks. And indeed, within moments, he can be seen down below, now nearer to those watching. A few voices call out:

"It's not a man riding, but a woman."

Others shout, "It's not a woman; it's a girl."

Avshalom looks hard and recognizes her.

"Bruria!"

He calls to the children:

"It's Bruria, the grandchild of the old man who gave us the camel and the cow and the barley. She has surely come to collect her debt. But why has she come without the old man? Perhaps he is behind her and in a moment he too will appear."

He goes on: "Dear friends are coming to visit us. We must receive them hospitably. I'll run to meet them and you wait here."

He runs a few steps, then stops and calls back, "David, come with me. You also know them."

They hurry on their way toward the guest.

They meet her in the valley. Avshalom puts out his hand and says, his face beaming with joy: "How are you, Bruria? Blessed be thy coming."

"How are you, Avshalom, and David. Blessed be the Lord who brought me to you in peace."

She jumps off the donkey, and holds out her hands to her good friends.

"Where is your grandpa?" asks Avshalom. "Is he coming along more slowly behind you?"

"Grandpa . . ." Bruria bursts out crying.

"Why are you crying, Bruria? What has happened?"

"He died."

"When? How?"

"Three weeks ago. He wanted very much to visit you, but his strength was spent. For three months he lay mortally ill . . ."

"May his memory be blessed. He was a dear old man."

"There are not many like him," says Bruria, as she wipes her tears.

"Come, Bruria. Let us go. Not far from here are all the children waiting to meet you."

The three start out, but then they see the children running down in a crowd. They have been too impatient to wait for the visitor. After all for a whole year they have not seen a new face. It has been as though they were isolated on an island in mid-ocean. Now Bruria has come, the girl who sent them broad beans, lentils, honey and salt. Now she has come to them. With eyes sparkling, crowding and jostling, they come running down and surround the guest.

Bruria stands stock-still. With wondering eyes she looks at the merry group of children, so healthy and excited. She wants to say something, but, overwhelmed, her words stick in her throat, and she cannot utter them.

"So this is the family . . ." she manages to say at last, and tears, shining like crystals, roll down her cheeks.

Everyone stops chattering, and stands hushed, touched to

the heart. Avshalom manages to master his feelings, and says: "Let us go to the fig orchard. There we'll sit down and you can have a real feast."

The whole assembly moves along, the children clustering around the guest. Each child is lost in thought. Nafthali, who is walking near Esther, whispers to her: "Essie, sing something."

"I'm shy."

"Don't be silly. You begin, and we'll join in."

So in the midst of the utter quiet, a soft voice is heard:

"In field and in valley
The little ants carry."

They all sing in unison:

"In insects and leaves
The living soul breathes."

When they reach the fig orchard, they settle under a shady tree, Bruria in the center with the children around her. Dinah sorts out the best figs, puts them in front of Bruria, and brings a jug of water: "Do eat and drink, Bruria."

"I am thirsty after my long journey."

She lifts the jug and drinks her fill. As she puts it down, she raises her eyes and sees the little heads close together. Avshalom says somewhat embarrassedly:

"Listen, Bruria, and forgive me if I am saying the wrong thing. Like us, you are an orphan, with no father and no mother, and without your dear old grandfather. What will you do in your village, forsaken and all alone? Let our family be your family. Be like a sister to us and we will be brothers and sisters to you. Live with us. Your fate will be our fate."

Tens of pairs of eyes gleam with surprise and joy. Miriam is the first to cry out: "Yes, be our sister, Bruria."

Dinah adds: "We have heard so much about you, Bruria! It was you that sent us the broad beans and the lentils, the honey and the salt. If only you could have seen the happiness, when we cooked pottage of lentils for the first time! If only you had seen the joy of the tiny children when they licked the sweet honey! Stay with us. We all love you."

Avshalom goes on: "What your old grandfather did and what you did, we can never forget. Without the camel, we could not have sown and plowed; without the cow and her milk, we could not have saved the children from serious illness. Nor could we have planted our barley. Stay with us!"

Bruria blushes.

"Do not talk about a debt. It was my grandfather's gift to you. After you left, he said, 'Instead of a sacrifice to the Temple, and the contribution of a tithe to the priests and Levites, I dedicate and devote a tithe and a contribution to the orphans of Vale-of-Figs.' And now you have offered me a home. Of course I will come to be your sister. I can bring something, too. There is the rest of grandfather's property, which he left me; twenty-two sheep, four cows, a camel, donkey, field produce. What shall I do with it? Tomorrow we'll go back to my village, and bring my poor possessions here."

Bruria's words cast a solemn silence on the group. But Gideon, son of Yehudah, who is only four, exclaims joyfully: "Another camel! This year, I too will plow with a camel."

And they all burst out laughing.

19

The days of winter come, and the work in the fields increases steadily. They go down to the valley to plow and sow with a camel hitched to each plow; even the two cows are harnessed to plows and they plow too. The cultivated fields are now increased many times in size. Vegetables are also planted. It is Bruria who obtains different kinds of vegetable seeds for them. She knows a great deal about growing vegetables, and teaches the other girls how to sow and plant. She also supervises the thinning out, the weeding and the hoeing.

On the fair days between rains, the children rise early. Some go out to sow; some to the vegetables, others to hoe around the vines. A few girls stay behind in the houses to cook and wash, to mend and sew. Now even the younger children begin to work, among them those who, a year before, played hide-and-seek and other games. This year, they are already carrying some of the workload.

After the first rainfall, there is no rain for three consecutive weeks. The days are fine, bright and comfortable for working. During these weeks, they finish sowing the crops and vegetables, and weeding the vineyards. They have only just completed the planting when heavy rains begin to fall without a stop. Clouds and rain, thunder and lightning! They shut themselves up in the houses and do nothing. They only cook, eat, chat idly and sleep.

It is on one such rainy day, when the windows of the heavens are opened and the drops of rain join together and come streaming down like sheets of water that Avshalom says: "We are doing nothing. Our time is being frittered away. The small children are growing up without learning. They do not know the Bible stories or the words of the Prophets. We would do well if on such idle days we were to teach the younger ones chapters of the Bible and the Prophets."

"Well spoken, Avshalom," says David.

"Who will teach us?" says a child of seven.

"There is no one who knows the Scriptures as well as Elchanan does. He is really learned."

Elchanan blushes and comments:

"Why exaggerate, Avshalom? You were also considered a good pupil."

"Good. I too will teach them. But I am busier than you. It is better that you should be the teacher."

That very day, school begins. Elchanan teaches the little ones the alphabet. He draws the letters with chalk-stone on a board, explains and revises, explains and questions, until little by little, he accustoms them to add syllable to syllable, and to join them together to form a word.

"Look. This is ALEPH. After it comes BET, and then ALEPH again. We join them and you have a word ABA (father). Or for example, GESHEM (rain). How would you write that? We write first of all the letter GIMEL (G); after that letter SHIN (SH). If we join them, we have . . . ?"

Esther jumps up and calls out:

"I know. The two letters join together and we'll call that GESH . . ."

"If so, tell me, Essie, what letter must we add to make the whole word GESHEM?"

"NUN (N)."

"If so, what will you call the word?"

"GESHEN."

The children laugh. One of them shouts:

"I know. Add LAMED (L)."

"Silly," remarks another child. "With LAMED, the word will be GESHEL."

The children push each other with excitement, and Elchanan says:

"It's very simple. If you add MEM (M), then you have GESHEM."

"That's right!"

"I thought it was MEM but I was too shy to say so."

"Never mind. After a few days, you'll all know writing and reading . . ."

Elchanan is a patient teacher and the children quickly and easily acquire for themselves the secret of reading and writing. But Avshalom's method of teaching is different. He tells them from memory the stories and legends of the Torah, the sacred writings, and the history. The children listen, all ears, and drink in his sweet words. One of the stories interests them deeply:

". . . And after the destruction of Jerusalem and the burning of the Temple, the best of Jerusalem's people were exiled to Babylon. Among them was the King Zidkiyahu, whose sons were slaughtered before his eyes, and then his eyes were gouged out so that he was blind for the rest of his days. Our land was deserted. Only the remnant of Judah dwelt there and appointed over them was Gedaliah, son of Achikam, a descendant of King David, and one of the important officers. Fifty years after the day of the destruction of the city of Jerusalem there rose King Cyrus, who said to the Jews in his land: 'You are permitted to return to your country, to raise up the ruins, to build the Temple, and to be as all other peoples.' He brought the vessels of the Temple from his treasuries and returned them to them, and even gave orders to his army to protect them on their way through the desert from hostile nations . . ."

Little Jonathan, who is seven, asks: "And when will the Romans allow us to build the Temple?"

"The hour will come, the hour of redemption, and Jerusalem will be rebuilt, and the Temple will be built. And Israel will once again be a nation living in freedom."

Little Gideon, son of Yehudah, who is also sitting and listening asks: "And then will my father come back?"

"Of course. All the slaves will be freed."

"My father and my mother, too?"

"All of them."

"When?"

"I am not a prophet, and not the son of a prophet. God in His Heaven will have mercy on us and the redemption will come."

"Aren't there prophets now as there were long ago?"

"I don't know. Maybe."

Avshalom continues his story about the return to Zion from Babylon, and, when he finishes, Gideon asks:

"When will you tell us about Judah the Maccabee? You promised."

"Soon."

"And about the Laws?" asks one of the older children.

Avshalom tries to put into words his understanding of the Laws and the Ten Commandments, and the fierce defense of the Jewish way of life against the Romans, who sought conquest, and instituted slavery, idolatry and the arena. The Jews were for morality, for seventh-year rest and Jubilee, for the rights of the poor to gleaning in field and in crop, for the protection of orphan and widow; they forbade usury and interest, protected the Sabbath, and the right to rest, and the obligation to grant rest to laborer and working beast. "Therefore," Avshalom concludes, "even though the Romans conquer, it is Jerusalem and the Law that are eternal and will be victorious."

One rainy day, as the children cluster around, Avshalom and the older children tell the little ones of life in their village in former days. "Two or three times a year," they say, "a caravan of people would organize themselves to visit the nearest town. This was the most exciting event of the year. Mostly they would go after the threshing, or before a festival. The preparations would go on for weeks. Everyone would discuss every detail of who was going, what they should sell and buy, and how to guard against highwaymen, and take care not to be duped in the towns. Sick people joined the caravan to ask advice of physicians.

"The night of the departure, at midnight, the whole village would rise, the children too. They would make a great bonfire near the carob tree, and here men and women would stand, loading the produce on the camels and donkeys—pressed figs, sacks of barley and wheat, hens on top of all. The adults loaded the sacks and bundles, pitchers and skin bottles, and tightened the ropes, while the children played and jostled and made merry. At dawn the caravan set out. First the camels, walking importantly, listening to the tinkling of the bells around their necks; behind them, the donkeys, their gait confused and disorderly; then followed the whole crowd on foot, with only the sick and some women riding on donkeys.

"The caravan would move off into the distance and those left behind would watch with envy the lucky ones going off to the wide world. As the sun rose, the villagers could still see the caravan making its slow way along the narrow path among the rocks, appearing and disappearing as the path twisted and wound around the hill opposite. Finally it disappeared for the last time behind the mountain. 'God speed! Safe return!' they shouted. Then followed for those left behind days and weeks of waiting. They talked of nothing but the caravan, speculating about its journey, its sales and purchases, and when it would return.

"When it came, the whole village was filled with joy, and there was a great hustle and bustle. Those who returned showed off their city purchases; the children received their presents in noisy excitement, mostly beautiful flutes from Damascus. They talked of the journey, of the tall houses in the cities, of the market and its wonderful wares, of the circus. The other villagers repeated the stories over and over for many a long day."

For about a month, the rains and mud drag on. No work is done in the fields or vineyards or gardens. All these days the lessons and stories and legends continue. On one of the fine days, when the earth has dried and it is possible to plow and to hoe, Avshalom says:

"Tomorrow we're going out to work. The weeds have sprung up in the vineyards. We'll plow and we'll hoe."

Jonathan jumps up and asks anxiously, "And our studies?"

"We won't stop them. On fine days, too, Elchanan will teach the little ones for an hour or two."

"And will you stop your nice stories?"

Avshalom is perplexed. He thinks and then answers: "Our sages said, 'If there is no flour, there is no learning.' If I and others like me do not work, we shall again go hungry as we did last year. Therefore, it will be on the Sabbath that I shall tell you stories from the Bible and the legends of our sages of blessed memory. Next Sabbath, I'll tell you all about the Sabbath; how God took the Sabbath out of His stores and gave it as a gift to the Children of Israel."

"Oh, good, good!"

And indeed Avshalom devotes most of the Sabbaths to stories from the Bible and to legends. The very first of his stories is about the Kings of the House of David. Not only the little ones listen, but the big children of his own age sit and listen with flashing eyes.

20

Winter passes and summer comes; it too passes without incident. Once again the children harvest the grain and thresh it, harvest grapes and figs, and dry raisins. Now they also have beasts to take to pasture. In the spring, the sheep drop their lambs, and the cows too have their calves, male and female. The flocks require not a little attention—pasturing, milking, shearing. But the small children have grown, and in the fields it is not the bigger ones who do the work, but the former little ones among the family of children. Jonathan and Esther become shepherds on a permanent basis. Both of them learn to play the flute. The smallest of the children join them, as they also want to help with the work in the fields, and their wish is granted.

Avshalom carries a far greater burden than the others. Besides the ordinary work of harvesting or sowing which he does like the others, he is the one who buys and sells, and in accordance with his decision, things are marketed; in every quarrel or fight, he is the judge and arbitrator. As for work schedules, and deciding what has to be done, he is the one elected to do this as well. He is the manager, the counselor, the guide, the older brother, the father.

But in the very few moments of repose that he has, when the children are lying down and resting after the day's toil, he is tormented by memories of the past, and he worries about their future life together. Not for a single moment does he forget his parents in exile, in serfdom. Who knows what has happened to them? Maybe at the very hour that he and his comrades are free to go as they please, his father and mother are serving as slaves to a Roman or Greek? And Rachel, his beloved friend—she who was like his sister, with whom he had played together from his earliest infancy—where was she? He remembers how he used to play his flute for her. Rachel . . . How happy he would be if only she were here, working at all the different tasks, listening to his stories on the Sabbath, with her great eyes dreaming, lost in thought. . . . She would sit with him in the moonlight and sing her lovely songs. What is her fate? Has she been sold as a maidservant? Maybe God released her from the fetters of slavery and on her way into exile she died, and was buried in the sands of the desert? Rachel . . . Rachel . . .

Avshalom tries to shake off his sorrowful thoughts and to concentrate on pleasant things, such as what they have planted in the fields, and their hopes of a great surplus of produce. He decides eventually that when he has a great deal of money, he and a few of his friends will go to look for his parents and the other captives.

He will find them and will redeem them and Rachel and the other captives with the money, and they will all return together to Vale-of-Figs, and work and live together ever after. He continues daydreaming.

He is now fourteen years old. In another two or three years he will be a young man, and so will some of the others. The little "kids" in the group are fast becoming little goats. In a few years, all these children will be reaping and harvesting, plowing and working as shepherds. The congregation of children will become a large village, a congregation of adult men and women.

But he determines that when they are grown up, they will still not say "mine" and "yours," but "ours"; they will still be like sisters and brothers, one big family, one complete group with not one of its parts separate. They will do away with individual houses, and will erect one large building with many rooms, which can accommodate all the members of the family. This house will have three storys, and will stand at the top of a hill, like a beacon visible from a great distance, and will be well fortified against enemies and robbers.

Under the house, there will be storerooms, granaries and closets for produce and fruit. The vineyard will also be a single large one. Some vines, old and neglected, which give little fruit, will be uprooted, and young vines planted in their place.

During the day, Avshalom appears a very practical person, not at all given to daydreaming, but diligent and wide-awake. In his free time, however, he wanders along the paths of his imagination, along the lanes of dreams and reverie

In the third summer, when members of the oldest group have turned fifteen and have grown into youths and maidens, tall, sturdy and lovely to look at, Avshalom stands before them one Sabbath and says: "Until now we have been accustomed to talk about the past. Now the time has come to talk about the future."

The children are wide-eyed with wonder.

Avshalom does not beat about the bush but simply comes to the point.

"Until now, we have lived in several houses, a few of us in each house. Now we are growing older. These houses are not enough for us. Besides they are no longer strong. If robbers should attack us, they would not be proper protection for us. Let us rather build one big house with many rooms, so that we can all live in it together. The house will stand on top of the hill, and will be fortified. On the first floor, there will be storerooms for grain. Yes, it is a tremendous undertaking, but the little ones are growing bigger, and they will help us. I know that we shall not complete it in one month, not even in the summer months shall we finish such a huge task. It will take two or three years, especially if we build a large house and fortify it. We have stones in plenty from the ruined houses and also enough gravel and lime."

They are taken aback at Avshalom's words. No one has thought of this before, and so there are many doubts and much hesitation.

"Will we really be able to put up such a big building by ourselves?" asks Miriam. "Besides, we are needed for all the other work."

"What will become of the houses?" queries David. "Will we smash them down? After all, they are still good buildings."

"Maybe it is better to build two or three smaller houses," comments Tamar, "and be done with it. Why do we want such a tremendous building?"

Elchanan adds, "What Avshalom says is all very well, but who here knows enough about building to be able to erect such a structure?"

Some of them, however, are impressed by Avshalom's proposal. Nafthali is most enthusiastic.

"It is a wonderful idea! There are so many stones and no shortage of working hands. My father, as you know, was an expert builder, and I learned a little at his side."

When everyone has had his say, Avshalom rises, his face glowing with excitement and his voice keen with enthusiasm.

"Brothers and sisters, big and small," he cries. "I have listened to all your questions, but there is one question that must be considered first of all. Have you thought about how you would like to live in the future? Do you want us, even after we grow up, to be one family, one congregation, like we are now, or is each to live in his own house, and work in his own field and vineyard? If we are to take the second way, then Tamar is right. It is better to put up two or three houses, but if we are to follow the first path and decide we will always be one body and one soul, then

'ROYAL' DEVIL COIN BOX

SECRET — Coin rattled in box (up and down) forces bottom section out.

IMPORTANT — Should you eject inner section completely — reinsert partially. THEN TWIST UNTIL YOU HEAR A CLICK — it is then in proper position. DO NOT USE FORCE!

PRESENTATION — Borrow a quarter from spectator asking him to remember date. Rattle box hard to show that coin is inside. The bouncing coin pushes out secret section just enough to form a slot for coin to pass through. Hold coin box so that *only ejected portion is not shown.*

Now permit coin to slide secretly into hand, and immediately after, close compartment. Keep coin in closed hand. Place box on back of same hand and inform spectator you are going to cause the coin to penetrate box and hand. Tap box and at same time, drop the coin.

A Good Magician Never Revea[illegible]e Secret.

No single trick makes a[illegible]gician.

Your popularity grows with [illegible]ollection.

See the many other tricks [illegible]dealer.

we must erect a large building for all of us. Do you understand? That is the question that we must answer first of all."

Bruria is the first to rise to her feet, and she begins softly, but her words become more and more fiery, and gradually win them over:

"What are we today? Just orphans, children whom fate has forced to live together like one big family. During the first difficult years, we drew closer to each other, and learned to join together; our roots interlaced and intertwined until they have become one root, with one stem. Now, after we have become accustomed to this, I ask you: Why should not other people live this way? Do we eat less than we would if each lived alone and for himself? This way of life uproots hatred and jealousy, and competition and strife, and why" (here she raises her voice passionately) "should not the other villages also live as we do? Is there any reason why we should not return to the way of life of our early ancestors? My good old grandfather used to tell me that many generations ago the whole tribe lived as one family. If they slaughtered an ox, everyone ate; if they hunted an animal, they made a bonfire and all members of the tribe sat around and enjoyed it. So I say: Let us continue as we started, and go from strength to strength. We'll put up a big house and never again will there be 'mine' and 'yours.' "

Her words, expressed so forcefully and passionately, have an effect. The children stand up one after the other and support her, and there is not a single person who disagrees. Then Avshalom gets up, and, with a pleasant smile, asks: "And what about the big house?"

"We'll build it!"

"One house for all of us!"

"A fortified house against enemy and robber!"

"This very summer, after the grape harvest, we'll lay the cornerstone."

"Yes, this summer!"

"Nafthali will be the head builder and we'll all be his assistants."

"I'll haul stones on the donkey," says Gideon, now six years old.

21

For the first time since Bruria's arrival, new faces appear in the village. One morning, two people come, a master and a slave, the master riding on a mule, the slave on foot. The children are afraid. Stopping next to one of the good houses, the man dismounts from his mule and hands the reins to his slave. He stretches to his full height, straightens his back after his tiring ride, and asks one of the children: "Who is the head man of this village?"

The child is confused and does not understand what he means.

The man repeats: "Who is the elder of this village?"

Still the child is silent.

"Are you dumb? Where is your father?"

The child runs to a nearby house and shouts: "Avshalom! Avshalom!"

When Avshalom saw the rider from afar, his face had darkened. Now when he is called, he comes, his heart gloomy and full of foreboding. He presents himself to the visitor and says: "Here I am."

"I want to see the village elder."

"There is no elder among us."

"Then where are the adults?"

"There are no adults among us."

"Who are you, and who are the inhabitants of this village?"

"We are war orphans."

"Who is looking after you?"

"We are looking after ourselves."

Reluctantly Avshalom is forced to tell the visitor all about the children and their work, and how they are living. The visitor is astonished and remarks:

"This is the first time in my life that I have seen or heard of such a thing!"

He goes from house to house, and looks around, and chats with some of the children, who have collected and are staring at him, half afraid, half interested. At last he says to Avshalom: "As far as I can see, although you are only a boy of fifteen or so, you are the elder of this village. So I address myself to you. I am the appointed tax collector of the Romans. The other villages have been paying their tax from the time of the conquest, but your village was thought to be destroyed and deserted, and so it was passed over. Only by chance did I get to know that there was life here. From afar a flock of sheep was seen and I was sent here. You have to pay me three whole years' tax."

Avshalom's face blanches. He responds earnestly: "Bear with me, sir. The first year we starved. We got through the year after that with great difficulty, and only this year do we have a little produce. If you take it away, we shall die of starvation."

"It is an imperial decree. I have no power to change it."

"It is a decree for our destruction!"

The envoy softens somewhat and says: "I'll only collect the tax for this year."

So saying, he begins to calculate how much wheat, barley, wine and oil they are obliged to give him.

Again Avshalom's face falls and he pleads:

"There are nearly sixty of us. Only about twelve boys and girls are fourteen or fifteen years of age. We have to work and to provide for almost sixty people."

The man becomes angry and rebukes Avshalom: "Don't be impudent, boy. The Romans levy a tax rental on me, and you come and make things difficult for me. I have already let you off two years' tax."

Avshalom's face becomes expressionless and he answers not a word. He only bites his lips and remains silent.

That very day, the produce is weighed for paying the tax. The master and his slave leave it all in one heap and the visitor informs them: "I'll send camels to take this load."

Before he leaves the village, the visitor inquires artlessly: "Haven't you any surplus to sell?"

"We would have sold a little wheat, wine and olives."

"Good. I'll send you a buyer."

A few days later, a man comes riding up on a donkey.

He takes a warm interest in the fate of the children. He buys their surplus produce and pays them in coin of silver and gold. When Avshalom puts the money away in a safe hiding place, he thinks: "The beginning of the ransom for the captives."

The next summer, the fourth year after the destruction, the tax collector comes again, and with him the merchant.

The one takes, the other pays. The secret ransom hoard increases.

22

At the end of the summer, as soon as the decision is made to put up the big building, the children set to work. Before the rains come, they manage to level the hilltop, and remove the rocks. With the help of the two camels and the donkey, they haul hewn stones from the ruins of the houses to the building site. The distance is short and in a day they load and unload many times. The children of nine and ten are able to help with this work. They roll the stones, and even help to load when the stones are small. The actual work of transport is the responsibility of the little children. They lead the animals when bringing the rock, and return riding on them.

By the sowing season, several large heaps of stones have piled up near the building site. The digging of the foundations is planned for the winter days when the earth is soft and easier to work. Indeed, it is only in the month of Shvat, with its heavy rains, and after the sowing and hoeing around the vines have been completed, that they begin digging. While some dig, others take the earth away in baskets. Here and there they encounter rock. The work is not easy for boys of fifteen and a half, and it takes longer than they expect at first. They hope to build the foundations before the barley harvest, but in this they are disappointed. Besides the fact that the digging takes so much longer than anticipated, there is other work which holds them up—such as pruning the vines, hoeing, sowing sesame seed—and by then, it is time for the barley harvest. So they are forced to leave the digging until after the harvest and the threshing.

As soon as they have completed the work in the fields, the building begins in earnest with great enthusiasm and diligent work. Even the girls do this hard work, and even the small children help with the lighter tasks. Nafthali is the head builder. At first, he makes numerous mistakes. He is compelled to build and destroy, and build over again, but each mistake schools him in an aspect of the work and teaches him precision in his workmanship, until he learns the trade in its finer details and gradually becomes more experienced.

That summer they manage to do a good deal. The foundations are laid, and the first story is built. This is the one designed as storerooms for grain and fruit, and for storage of tools. It is only when the first story is erected that most of the defects in building become apparent. The walls are very thick and strong, and indeed could stand for hundreds of years, but one wall is not quite straight. In the middle there is a bulge of several stones, which project like a belly, for they have not been laid in the true vertical. Another wall is concave in one part. It is true that it is possible to level it out with plaster but, nevertheless, it is a mistake. The small windows have not been placed at the same height all around; one is higher, one lower. These faults upset Nafthali and if he had been permitted, he would have pulled the whole building down and rebuilt it from scratch. He vows to himself, "With the second story, I'll be seven times more exacting. I'll measure each detail; I'll test every step and weigh what has to be done. I'll take my time and think it out and not hurry until I know for certain that what I have built is as it should be and absolutely correct!"

With the sowing season, the building comes to a halt, for field work takes precedence over everything else. That winter, Avshalom carries out his idea of the large vineyard. The slope of the hill to the south is cleared of stones, holes are made and new vines planted. These new vineyards and the additional fields sown mean increased work.

This is the fifth winter after the destruction, and of their life as one large family. For the first time, all the fields are under cultivation. The flocks increase and keep no fewer than four children constantly occupied. On the hill, the building rises, with a story that has not as yet been plastered. On the southern slope of the hill is the large vineyard in the early stages of development. Vegetables grow in plenty. The babies too grow apace, growing bigger and taller. Little Esther, the singer, is already eleven; Avshalom and his age group are entering their seventeenth year (which is a lucky number homiletically) and Gideon the son of Yehudah is already eight years old, a fine, sturdy boy, and considered an excellent shepherd. The work goes full steam ahead. From dawn until sunset everyone toils and labors. Even in the stormiest rains, they do not rest. They find other work in the new building, especially inside the rooms, leveling the ground, plastering inside, removing superfluous stones. But the rainy days are also reserved for studies. Elchanan now does no other work than teaching. The youngest group of five- and six-year-olds are learning their alphabet and the group above them is already studying chapters in the Torah of Moses.

Thou shalt not steal . . . Thou shalt not kill . . .

Elchanan is explaining the content and deep meaning of the Ten Commandments to his class. At this time, the younger group is playing outside. The sun is warm. On the slope of the hill, the earth is already dry, and it is possible to run and jump and play hide-and-seek. The children play and get into mischief, and they sing and laugh. All at once, they gather underneath the window and listen to Elchanan's voice as he teaches the older class.

"Honor your father and your mother . . ."

They crowd under the tree near the house and little Dvorah asks:

"Tell me, what is 'father'? I have never seen one." Little Gedaliah repeats the question. "Yes, yes. What is 'father'? And what is 'mother'?"

Joseph is the biggest of them, and he is the one who explains:

" 'Father' is a big, big man, taller than Avshalom and Elchanan."

"And 'mother'?"

" 'Mother' is a tall woman, big, beautiful, and she kisses the small children, hugs them and puts them to sleep, and sings them songs and tells them stories."

"Like Miriam, Dinah, Bruria and Tamar?"

"Yes, like them, but bigger than they are, and older."

"Joseph, is it true that I have a father in Damascus?"

"And I have a mother, far away . . . ?"

"Joseph, where is Damascus? Behind this mountain? Isn't it?"

"My brother Jonathan told me that we have a mother and father, far away in Damascus or in Rome. You have to ride twenty days and twenty nights to get there, and on the way there are very high mountains and rivers and deserts and lots of robbers."

"When will we see them?" asks one small child sadly.

"When we grow big, we'll have lots of horses and then we'll ride there."

"Will I also ride? Will you take me with you? I also want to see my father and my mother," Gedaliah implores.

One child, whose parents were killed, asks:

"But isn't Avshalom father?"

"He is not a father. He is our big brother."

"And Elchanan?"

"Elchanan is also our big brother, also Nafthali, also David, also . . ."

"And Miriam, is she mother?"

"Miriam is our big sister, also Bruria, Dinah and Tamar. They are all our big sisters."

"And what are we?" asks little Dvorah.

"We are all of us little brothers and sisters."

"There are only brothers and sisters," remarks Gedaliah, the youngest of them all. "One big family of brothers and sisters. Avshalom is the biggest and I am the smallest, and you are all in the middle."

They all burst out laughing.

"Joseph, why do the big brothers and sisters work all the time and we little ones always play and don't do anything?"

"Because they are big and strong and can work and we are small and weak."

"I also want to work," shouts Shimon. "Avshalom told me once that we should all help each other, and we don't help at all."

"Do you know what?" Joseph decrees with enthusiasm. "The big ones are clearing stones from a piece of land for planting a vineyard, and they are building a house and growing vegetables. We'll also clear stones from a portion of ground and we'll plant a vineyard and look after some seedbeds and we'll also work."

"Hurrah! We'll clear stones from the small piece of ground at the edge of the wood near the rocks. We'll plant a vineyard there and we, the small ones, will have a vineyard."

"We'll also make a little house out of stone."

"We'll also make beds and plant carrot and radish."

"Oh, really lovely! The big ones will have a vineyard,

and the smaller ones a vineyard. They'll have a house, and we'll have a house, and we'll also have vegetables."

And all of them, jubilant and full of high spirits, run to the edge of the wood and begin to clear stones from the ground.

23

What is happening meanwhile in the Land of Israel as a whole? Vespasian, who has become Caesar of Rome, is one of those men who love money. He issues a decree concerning the Land of Israel. "This is my property." And, having decreed thus, he begins to sell sections to those who offer the best price. His son Titus, after destroying Jerusalem, sheds rivers of blood there. He leads tens of thousands of people into captivity and sells many of them as slaves. Others he presents as gifts to his numerous friends in neighboring countries. Many are sent to work in quarries in far-off Corinth and in Egypt.

The strongest of the young men, the best looking and most courageous, are sent to entertain the imperial court of Rome and her population in the arena. At every Roman festivity, such as the birthday of the Emperor or of one of his sons, entertainment and sport are organized in the form of contests between ferocious wild beasts and the young men from Israel. At these festivities, thousands of young men are seized and torn limb from limb in front of the people of Rome; refined Roman matrons feed their eyes on the spectacle of blood spurting like water, stamp their feet with joy, clap their hands and laugh.

After the Destruction of Jerusalem and the Temple, three fortresses still remain that have withstood the enemy and do not succumb. They are very distant, in the vicinity of the Dead Sea, and across the Jordan River. Titus at first thinks it is not worthwhile to travel so far in order to conquer them: he believes that the resistance of these fortresses is nothing but the last death throes of a nation.

Instead he arranges celebrations and festivities, spectacles. The slain heroes of Judah are still unburied, but Titus makes merry in Caesarea on the shores of the Mediterranean. Two thousand five hundred of the precious sons of Zion fall in these "sports" of the Romans. As he passes through cities and capitals of different nations and tribes on his way home to Rome he organizes entertaining spectacles for them too, so that they may witness his victory over Israel.

But when he is appointed by Vespasian Basus the prefect of the Land of Judah, he is urged to conquer the last three fortresses. For three more years the war drags on between him and the last of the Zealots.

He conquers the fortress of Rhodeon first. The fortress Macorus, however, on the far side of the Jordan, built in the days of Alexander Jannai, has natural protection in the deep valleys which surround it. Several thousands of the heroes are in it, led by a man of great daring, Eleazar. Not only do the Romans find it impossible to take this fortress, but Eleazar and his men from time to time actually carve their way through to the Roman camp and create havoc there.

But at last fortune turns her face on Eleazar, and he falls into the hands of the Romans. They stand in full view of the fortress and torture Eleazar before the eyes of his defenders. They cannot bear to witness his sufferings, and surrender.

Even after the conquest of this fortress, a last remnant of courage remains, and that is in the mighty fortress of Masada. This fortress is situated on the high mountains that lie piled around the Dead Sea.

The fortress stands on a lofty rocky peak, the ascent of which is fraught with great danger. The leader of the defenders of this fortress is another Eleazar, the son of Yair. Those in the fortress have a large supply of food. His Zealots defy the Romans who besiege them, and years pass before the Romans manage to force a breach in one of the walls. The inner wall, which is built of wood, is set alight when the Romans project flaming materials from their camp below. In their last hour, when the besieged and Eleazar at their head realize that within a short while they will fall into Roman hands, they declare: "We shall die by our own hands rather than fall into the hands of the Romans." When the Romans burst into the fortress, they find only five people alive.

And the year is the third after the Destruction of Jerusalem.

The heroes of Judah who manage to escape to neighboring countries fire the flame of revolt wherever they go. So the Jews rebel against the Romans in Alexandria, in Cyrenia, and other countries too. Every revolt is crushed in the end by the Romans with the greatest cruelty.

In the Land of Israel, there is no revolt during the first few years. And indeed, who is there to revolt? The slain? The young men who are captives and sold as slaves? Or those who remain, who are the old, the maimed, the orphans, the widows? And with what can they revolt? Sparsely populated, ruined, devastated, wretched and humiliated, their precious country lies spread beneath her lovely skies. Festive Rome is able to rule the country and her desperate survivors with but a handful of her soldiers.

During the years immediately after the Destruction and conquest of the Land of Israel, the star of Prince Julius Agrippa II, he who was considered King of the Jews of Galilee a few years before the Destruction, rises. A faithful slave of the Romans, he helped them with his counsel to overcome the Zealots, and even raised armies for the Romans. Most hated by the Zealots, he was regarded by them as a traitor. When the country is conquered and destroyed, Vespasian does not forget his ally and loyal slave, and expands the boundaries of Agrippa's kingdom to Mount Hermon and the whole district of Galilee. When Agrippa sees what he has achieved with his treachery, it may be that he feels the prickings of remorse, for he tries to strengthen the last remnant of survivors in his area and deals with them with some measure of kindness. He even intercedes for them in Rome in their hour of need.

When the sickly, prostrate remnants of Judah see the good deeds and tender ways of Agrippa, they forget his former ugly acts and forgive him, comforting themselves with the thought: "It is a spark of deliverance. Let us guard it and maybe we shall increase the spark into a great fire."

Vale-of-Figs, hidden among the mountains, is close to the area under the jurisdiction of Agrippa. But, to tell the truth, no one gives it a thought–not the Romans, not the Jewish ruler of Galilee. At the fixed time, the tax collector arrives and takes his due, but beside him, no person of the ruling section appears. The life of the community of children in the village, living according to its own unique system, continues without any interference. It is like an isle of green in the wilderness and desolation, like a special tribe among the sowers of destruction and ruin.

24

Passover. In three or four months it will be six years since the Destruction of the Temple, since the razing of Vale-of-Figs. Two weeks before the Festival of Passover, the children move into the new house, which stands like a small fortress among the peaks. On the first story are two large rooms which serve as storerooms for grain and fruit. The story above has five rooms for sleeping, a large dining hall, and a kitchen. Surrounding the house is an enormous courtyard, the fence of which is a wall of stone.

At first the children think the house will be really spacious, but when they actually move in to live in it, they realize that it could prove too small for them. If they sleep in the sleeping rooms only, they will be compelled to sleep ten or eleven in a room. So they have to make use of the large dining room to help the situation, and a few of them find themselves a corner on the terrace which faces west. There is now more space, more light and air than in the previous houses. Moreover, they are all together in one house, a matter of importance to a community of people whose work is one and whose lives are one. The very sight of the house, the fruit of their toil, fills them with enthusiasm and faith.

It is time for the barley harvest, and of course everyone is busy with it, so that no one can do what they really long to do—to fix up the house and perfect its appurtenances, and make it beautiful, so that it will gleam with brightness for the days of the Festival of Freedom. This is the first time since the Destruction that they prepare for the celebration of a festival, making all the detailed arrangements with much happiness.

On the eve of the Festival, most of the girls and the small children are busy decorating the large hall. On the walls, they hang a great deal of greenery, palm leaves, branches of fig and carob, sprays of vines, lilies and wild flowers, ears of barley and wheat. From the ceiling, they suspend tens of little oil lamps, so that every corner of the hall is brightly lit. On the long tables, they spread all the hangings and cloths which remain after the Destruction. On these, they place stone vases, containing lilies and other flowers. They even slaughter two young goats and bring jugs of wine in plenty; bake matzot, the flat unleavened bread of the Passover, with flour of selected wheat, and cook different kinds of special preserves with raisins and figs.

Although all these preparations are made with great merriment, it is mixed with feelings of sadness; they never forget the Great Chastisement of their nation or the sad fate of their parents.

They often talk about their parents in captivity, and a heavy gloom descends on them. Then they cannot suppress their tears.

But life is strong in them. It is like a mighty stream of water that overcomes all obstacles. Our sages have said: "It is decreed of the dead that they should be forgotten from the heart." And indeed, when the children are immersed in their work, it is as though their dead are forgotten, but on the festival days, in the midst of their happiness, a sigh escapes their lips. "Alas, why are our parents not sitting with us and making merry with us?"

A few hours before sunset, the children go down to the spring to wash and change into their festival clothes, and return home to their house, which shines with a wonderful, precious light. That evening, they all recline as the Passover custom requires and Avshalom narrates in his pleasant, warm voice the legends of the Exodus from Egypt. Between stories, there is eating and drinking—cabbage and raisins, onions fried in oil, glasses of wine—and over every glass, they say the blessing: "As we were redeemed from the exile of Egypt, and as we were redeemed from the exile of Babylon, so shall we be redeemed in our own day from the yoke of wicked Rome. Amen. Amen."

When the roast meat is served, a rare dish in Vale-of-Figs, tongues begin to wag in merry speech, like rivulets of water tumbling waywardly down hilly slopes. Between the roast and the vegetable pottage, they burst forth into a mighty flow of song, and the leader, as always, is Esther, now twelve, her voice stronger and sweeter than ever. She begins singing a folk song, and the others join in lustily, pouring themselves into the singing, so that echoes resound through the mountain ranges.

Since the Destruction of the Temple, these hills and valleys, these fields and rocks have not heard such a joyous outpouring of happy song. But, inevitably, in the end, a tone of sadness is fused with the gladness of the song; eyes are lowered as if in shame at their excessive joy. Tears flow and hearts are filled with sorrow.

Avshalom stands up and says: "We are happy, joyous, celebrating, dining, and in a little while we shall also begin to dance. But while we are enjoying ourselves so much, who knows the fate of our dear ones? Are they still living? And if so, who knows what suffering they are undergoing? Who knows where my father and my mother are now? Are they also sitting and celebrating the Festival of Freedom, or are they wallowing in a stable as slaves?"

He sighs deeply and tears come to his eyes. Restrained weeping breaks forth from the children and Avshalom continues: "And Yehudah ben Zakkai, the Shibbolite, the great hero, one of the heroes of Israel, what is your fate, Yehudah? Did you die in an arena, or, bound in chains, are you lying in a prison pit?"

When Gideon hears the name of his father mentioned by Avshalom, he bursts into bitter weeping, and a wave of sobs joins his weeping, but the voice of Avshalom goes relentlessly on: "And what is the fate of Menachem, father of Miriam; Shimshi, father of Jonathan; Nechama, mother of Esther, and all the others? And what is your fate, Rachel?

You could have been with us now. Why did God chastise you and cast you into the teeth of the wild beasts?" A sob breaks forth from his throat. He falls silent and sits down.

But then they come to the final part of the evening, the dance. It is as if the tears have cleansed them, purified them of sorrow. Their legs seem to get up of their own accord to dance. They dance in a confusion of jumping, prancing and hopping, with an enthusiasm that seeks to stifle their sorrow. The dancing continues for a long time. It is full of strong feeling, longing for the past and yearning for freedom.

Suddenly, in the midst of the boisterous dancing, there is the sound of knocking at the door, which they have left open, according to the Passover custom.

25

The dancing stops all at once. Instantly happiness fades and fear pierces their hearts. All faces turn to the door. In the doorway appears an old traveler, clad in rags, his face thin, his eyes sunken in their sockets, his whole being bespeaking weariness and utter sadness. The dust of the roads cakes his shabby clothes; his long beard covers his face; on his weary feet are old soles of leather, patched. As if the bright light in the hall is too intense for him, he shields his eyes with his right hand, looks left and right, and says in a loud whisper: "I thank Thee, oh God. They are Jews, my brethren, and not worshipers of idols."

Elchanan, standing near the door, says: "Blessed be your coming to the shadow of our roof."

The old man looks around quickly, astonished, excited: "What is this place? Who are you?"

The crowd stares at him, and he at them. The eyes of Miriam are fixed spellbound on the traveler. Suddenly, she cries out: "Father!"

The old man looks at her earnestly, searching, and then he says in a choked voice: "Can it be Miriam, my daughter!"

They fall into each other's arms, and the children crowd around them in a confused emotion. The old man is pale and moved, he keeps looking around him, and whispering: "I thank Thee, God . . . Miriam, my daughter, alive . . ." They bring him wine, food. He sips the wine, and at last he asks, "So you are the children from the cave?"

"Yes."

"And you are all alive?"

"Nearly all of us."

"Who built this place?"

"We did, with our own hands."

"I would have thought it the work of the Romans. A post for their armies."

The children see how tired he is. They restrain themselves and do not rain the questions upon him which are bursting from their lips.

The old man embraces Miriam his daughter again and again, kisses her hair, her forehead, her hands, laughs and then weeps. At last, Gideon, son of Yehudah, unable to restrain himself any longer, tugs at his cloak, and asks in a trembling voice: "And my father, where is he?"

The old man strokes his hair lovingly. "Whose son are you, dear boy?"

"Yehudah the Shibbolite, the great leader."

The old man sighs.

"So you are the son of Yehudah ben Zakkai, the hero? He lives, but he has suffered much. He was injured by wild animals in the spectacle that Titus organized on his way to Rome. He was thought dead, but in fact remained alive. When he recovered, he was sold as a slave to a Greek, who took him to Athens. From there he ran away twice, but each time he was caught and punished severely. About two years ago, I saw him in a village near Damascus. He was fettered and was working as a drawer of water."

He heaves a deep sigh and continues: "He has aged. Since the contest with the wild animals, the joints of his bones ache. His great dream is to escape."

Gideon turns aside, trembling, anguished.

Avshalom approaches the old man and asks: "Maybe you know the fate of my parents? Abraham . . ."

"Ah. You are Avshalom, his son. How big you have grown—and how handsome! A young man like a cedar. Your parents too were sold as slaves; they wandered from place to place with their master, a Roman tax collector. Last year, the officer left Syria, and went to Rome. He treated them well and freed them."

"Where are they now?" asked Avshalom, in simultaneous joy and terror.

"They hired a field for growing vegetables. If only they knew you were alive . . ."

Dinah too comes up and asks fearfully: "And my father and mother?"

"Who are they?"

Miriam answers for her: "Reuben, son of Moshe."

"Oh, since we left here, captives, in chains, I have not seen him. It seems he was in the convoy sent to Rome."

Dinah bursts into bitter weeping. There is a heavy, oppressive silence. All surround and try to comfort her, but Dinah cannot be comforted. She goes out onto the terrace to weep by herself.

Jonathan, standing near the visitor, wants to ask, but the words will not come. Miriam feels for him and she asks: "What happened to Shimshi, father of Jonathan?"

"Shimshi? May his memory be blessed. He was so handsome, so tall, so brave a soldier. I heard that he was killed in the arena. And your mother died two years later. So I heard."

Jonathan's hands begin to tremble. His face goes white. Bruria goes up to him, embraces him with great compassion.

Other children ask about their parents, but the old man cannot always give a clear answer. Then Miriam asks suddenly: "And you, Father, did you suffer very much?"

"This is not the time to tell all that I suffered, till I reached you."

The question about the fate of his little friend Rachel has been on the tip of Avshalom's tongue for some time. Yet he cannot bring himself to ask about her. Miriam glances at him and reads his feelings. She asks: "Father, maybe you know what happened to our good friend, Rachel?"

"Rachel, daughter of Tovim?"

"Yes, yes . . . she . . ."

"Her life is miserable and hard. She was sold as a maidservant. She is working at carpet-making in Damascus.

Some tens of women and girls work together with her, among them Sidonese, Egyptian, Samaritan, Syrian and Hebrew women. She is as beautiful as the sun but her lot is bitter."

Avshalom's face turns pale. Everyone is looking at him, and knows his sorrow. Miriam comes up to him and presses his hand. She draws him aside into a corner, and whispers: "Be strong, Avshalom."

Suddenly Avshalom's eyes glisten; his face reddens; his eyelids flutter. He takes a step forward and exclaims loudly: "Rachel shall come back to us. We must save her. My life is no life unless I bring Rachel back to our house."

The old man Menachem sits at the head of the table, eats of the best part of the roast, sips wine. He answers all of the questions he is asked, he tells terrible stories of the lives of the captives; crowding around him, emotional and furious, the children of Vale-of-Figs sit and listen.

PART THREE

THE SEARCH

26

That summer, after the harvest is completed, as well as the threshing and the gathering of the grapes, six years after the Chastisement, two youths and an old man set out on asses from Vale-of-Figs. They are Avshalom, Nafthali, and Menachem, Miriam's father. Their destination is Damascus.

It has been decided by vote to begin the attempt to redeem the parents. A start is to be made in Damascus, the nearest point. There they will make inquiries about the rest of the captives, and, even if they are compelled to travel to Rome, they will do so, in order to liberate them. All the surplus produce is sold that year. Part of the flocks is sold as well. The money which was hidden in the earth is added to the proceeds.

They have only just left the gates, seen off by the whole

crowd, when Gideon, son of Yehudah, who is nine, announces tearfully, "I want to go with you. My father is there. I must be the one to bring him back and save him."

"What are you talking about, Gideon? How can we take a child with us on a journey so long and so dangerous?"

"I am not so young. I won't worry you. You can ride and I'll walk."

"But the way is dangerous. There are brigands and murderers."

"It's the same for me as for you. I must go! I must go!" So saying he bursts into tears. Everyone is in a state of confusion. How can they permit a child of nine to go? But his weeping and his pleading tear at the heartstrings. There are those who side with him. Elchanan, for example, says: "Let him go. What harm will it do? Why is the danger greater for him than for you?"

Dinah joins him, claiming: "He may be nine, but his strength and his intelligence are like those of a boy of twelve. Let him go."

Finally Avshalom says, "All right, you can come with us, Gideon. Hurry and get him ready."

Miriam puts in additional provisions for the journey. The other children, his friends, help him to pack, hug and kiss him. Gideon, delighted, takes a long stick in his hand and runs ahead of the asses, so as to be first.

"Gideon, get on one of the asses."

"No. I'll walk. You ride."

"Little stupid. You won't be able to go all the way on foot. We'll take turns, and we'll change every once in a while."

"We'll see if I cannot go on foot."

Everybody laughs. Meanwhile, the hour of departure has arrived. Everyone calls after them:

"Good luck. May your journey be successful!"

"Good-by."

"Good-by, good-by, good-by!"

Avshalom and Nafthali are fine youths of eighteen, tall, strong and lithe, and the journey is not difficult for them. And Gideon does not tire. He is always wide-awake, jolly and quick. But the old man Menachem is sickly and feeble. His years of suffering in exile press heavily upon him, and the journey exhausts him to the extreme. The road to Damascus takes five full days. Their plan? They hope to redeem the captives in Damascus and its environs with the money. Before returning home, they will inquire about the rest of the captives, and will send them word that they will be freed.

This is their plan, but when they try to put it into practice, they encounter all sorts of unexpected obstacles.

At noon of the fifth day, they enter Damascus, a noisy, bustling city, with huge buildings, markets, fountains, its streets thronged with hundreds of people. The old man, Menachem, who is used to all this, pays no attention, but the three boys, setting foot for the first time in their lives in a large city, feel dizzy. It seems to them that they will get lost in the crowds; that their ears are deafened by the clamor.

Menachem leads them through streets and lanes for more than an hour, and then they stop at one of the yards in an out-of-the-way lane.

"In this inn, we shall rest," he says. "The innkeeper is a Hebrew from near Tiberias. He too is an exile. I know him."

"When will we reach the house of my father and mother?" asks Avshalom impatiently.

"Patience, Avshalom. We still have to find our way very carefully."

They put the asses in the yard, give them some barley and hay, as well as water, and go into the tavern. They enter a large room without furniture, in which all the guests sleep on rush mats. Menachem approaches the innkeeper, a man of about fifty, holds out his hand, and greets him. "How are you, Eli?"

"Ah, Menachem. Peace be with you. From where do you come?"

"From the Motherland. I found my daughter alive and well. The children of our village are all alive. These are three of them from my village."

"And what about Galilee?"

"In the whole of Galilee, angry feelings have subsided and Agrippa the Second is king of the whole district. He has repented his evil doings, does not levy high taxes, and is like a father to them all."

"Really?" Eli marvels. "The farmers plow and sow, are fruitful and multiply?"

"There are many effects of the Destruction, and the desolation is great. Many villages are still in ruins. But in those that were not destroyed, and where the people did not go into exile, life is returning to normal. Even there, there is mourning for the young men who died in their youth, or who were exiled. Those who remain, however, plow and sow, and even plant vineyards."

"So they plant vineyards, eh?"

"Yes, as I said, one does not experience trouble with the Romans in the district where King Agrippa is the ruler. They say Vespasian treats him like a friend, is extending his boundaries, and that he himself is a kindly king. His subjects love him."

"Perhaps you have heard of Kfar-Hitiah, the village where I was born, which lies above Tiberias. If I knew that there was any settlement at all there, I would return to my farm, although it was completely ruined and destroyed. I am tired of living in a strange land. I am tired of the empty life of a tavern."

"Perhaps, Eli, it is worthwhile to return to your farm in any case, although I have not heard anything about your village."

Meanwhile, new visitors enter, and the conversation stops. Menachem and his companions sit at the table, order food and wine and eat heartily. During the meal, Avshalom again cannot restrain himself and asks: "When will we find out where my parents live?"

"And my father?" asks Gideon.

"Do not think that it is an easy task. Damascus is a large city, with many gates, and hundreds of alleyways. Many gardens and vegetable fields surround it. I do not know its roads very well. But there is an exile from Judah in Damascus, who knew your father. He will be able to tell us."

"What about Rachel?"

"We'll ask about her, too."

Menachem wants his companions to rest for a few hours. He will go alone, but they will not agree to this. "Where you go, we go too," they insist.

The exile from Judah, who knew Avshalom's father, Abraham, is delighted to see them and makes them very welcome. Before they can find out about their parents, he asks innumerable questions about the Jews in the Land of Israel, and what they are doing, about the Roman customs, about the status of Jerusalem and especially about the Yeshiva founded at Yavneh by Yochanan ben Zakkai. Are there indeed students studying there? Are there many? The man, formerly a farmer and husbandman in Judah, has learned to be a goldsmith in Damascus, and ekes out a poor living from it.

"So you are the son of Abraham the Azati? It is a miracle from Heaven. He thinks you are dead. He told me that a little girl, who was taken into captivity, narrated to him how his son Avshalom was killed by a Roman the day after the destruction of the village."

Avshalom cannot control himself and asks impatiently, "Where do they live?"

"It is about ten months since I last saw them. Then they hired a vegetable field outside the city, on the eastern side, on the road to the village of Kalamah, on the border of the orchard belonging to the nobleman, Krasus. They were about to rent another field, but since then I haven't seen them and don't know what has happened to them."

Heavy sorrow darkens Avshalom's face.

"Perhaps there are other people who know exactly?"

"Maybe, my son. But I do not know of anyone. I'll give

you some advice. Take the road out of the city, which leads to the village of Kalamah, and continue until you reach the orchard of the nobleman, Krasus. There you will find the field. Maybe they are still there. If not, perhaps the new tenants will know something about them."

They leave the city, and tramp along for a good hour before they reach the large orchard of Krasus. They also find the field on its borders. But instead of Avshalom's parents, there is an old Syrian couple living in the hut. Menachem asks them in their own language: "Have you been here long?"

"From the days of the first rains."

"Where are the former tenants?"

"They left about three weeks before the first rains. Where they went, we don't know."

"What now?" asks Avshalom in despair.

Old Menachem understands his sorrow. He too is distressed and says:

"Another day or two . . . we'll find them. There are many Jews in this city. There are synagogues. We'll ask. We'll search until we find them."

When they return to Eli's inn, night has already fallen. Depressed and exhausted after their long journey, they stretch out on the mats in the guests' room and fall into heavy sleep.

The next day, after joint deliberations, Nafthali says: "Until we can find Avshalom's parents, let us look for Rachel, and see what we can do."

After much wandering about in the alleys and main streets, the visitors turn down one of the side streets, and there in front of them is a high stone house, surrounded by a wall. On the street side is a large shop, open so that one can see it is full of carpets of every color and size. Most of the carpets are folded, rolled and neatly piled. Some carpets are spread on the floor, on tables, on walls.

Officers and grand ladies, with their slaves behind them, enter the shop and begin choosing, feeling, bargaining. When the purchase is finally concluded, the slave heaves the carpet onto his shoulder and carries it away.

The shopowner is an old man, with a large paunch. His straight nose and black eyes tell he is a Greek. Avshalom and his friends stand around in the shop as if buying carpets, handling and examining them, and inquiring from the assistant if there are others. He smiles patronizingly at the country bumpkins before him, and asks: "Are there not enough carpets here?"

"We should like to choose another color."

"We have more storerooms full of carpets," says the assistant haughtily, "and others are being made in our workshop."

"Maybe we can find what we want in your workshop?"

"We do not allow everyone to enter the workshop," answers the clerk, laughing condescendingly. And he refuses to change his mind. Menachem and his companions realize that they will not be able to penetrate into the workshop, in order to see if Rachel is among the women working there. They leave the shop crestfallen.

At the entrance of the shop, they bump into another clerk, who looks at them closely and says in Hebrew: "Do you desire to buy something here?"

The visitors are delighted to find a brother Jew and Menachem stammers in reply: "Yes . . . we want to buy carpets . . . not carpets . . . like these. . . . We want to find out . . . Excuse me, sir. You are our brother . . . perhaps you can give us some advice . . ."

The clerk understands the hint, peeps inside to see whether his employer is listening, and whispers: "This evening, in the city garden. Next to the fountain."

All that day, they visit homes of acquaintances of Menachem, but no one can help them in their search.

27

In the evening they wait impatiently in the city garden for the clerk from the carpet workshop. When he arrives, he signals to them to follow him. They enter a tavern, and sit at a table in the far corner. The man calls the waiter, and tells him to bring them red wine. Then he says: "My brothers, sons of Israel. Take heed of what the wisest of men said: If a man has a worry, he will talk about it. I am from the place Charoshet Hagoyim and my name is Yoram. I was a trader in carpets. At intervals, I used to travel to Damascus, to Egypt; I even got as far as Persia.

"I brought carpets and sold them in Eretz Israel. When the revolt in Galilee broke out, I was here, and could not return. A few months before the conquest of Jerusalem, things were a bit quieter in Galilee and Emek Yezreel. I returned home, and to my great misfortune, found my house with its walls destroyed. All the carpets and hangings had been looted. My wife and children had gone to her father's house in Yokneam to wait until the fury of war had passed over. I returned to Damascus thinking that I would reopen my business; but, because of the war, the workshops stopped functioning. They stopped my credit, and I was ruined. I hired myself out as a shopworker in the workshop of the Greek, Krasus. My salary is a pittance, but better is work whose reward is little, than idleness with great hunger."

He pours wine into the goblets and exclaims: "Drink, my guests. Who are you, and what is your wish?"

Menachem decides to be open with him, and begins: "We were almost neighbors. From Vale-of-Figs, our village, to Charoshet Hagoyim is a matter of four or five hours on foot. Our village was destroyed. Some of the people were killed; some went into captivity. Only orphan children remained. They rebuilt the village, although all their parents were killed or taken as slaves. In the workshop where you serve, there is a girl working, a Hebrew girl, from our village, and we want to redeem her with money."

"In our workshop there are more than one hundred women and girls. Most of them were bought as maidservants. I and the other shopworkers also have practically no access to the workshop which is in the yard, kept closed with a padlock, and surrounded by a wall. At very infrequent intervals, one of us may enter for a few minutes, perform his mission, and return. I have heard that there are a number of Hebrew girls there, but it will be very difficult to redeem them, even with much money. Some of the

Jews living here have already tried to do so without success. You see, this is how the Greek Krasus thinks: 'Carpet-making is a fine art; my girls have been well taught and do the most beautiful work. For a new girl to learn the art thoroughly, takes a good year. My carpets have a good name in Rome, in Egypt, and in all the other countries. It cannot pay me to sell my girls.' Only very occasionally is one sold, and then for a sum enough to buy three girls!"

The faces of the guests drop, especially Avshalom's. Nafthali observes his extreme distress and says to Yoram: "We have to redeem her. Let them ask as much money as they like. We'll work even harder and increase our produce for the next five years as long as we manage to take her away from here."

Avshalom looks at Nafthali gratefully. Then he turns to the clerk as though awaiting an answer.

"Well," says Yoram, "we can only try. This is my advice. Tomorrow or the next day, one of you boys and the old man, who knows the language spoken here, should appear in the shop. Wear better clothes. The old man can address himself to Krasus with the words: 'My young lord wants to buy one of your girls as a maidservant. Perhaps you would like to sell one?' Since sales are low now, maybe my lord will take you into the workshop, and you can bargain, and buy the girl."

The next day, during the morning when the shop is almost empty, two customers appear in the shop, one a handsome young man, clad like the son of one of the wealthiest of merchants, and the other, an old man, with a wrinkled face, who gives the impression of being an old retainer.

Krasus sits at the table counting coins. Menachem and Avshalom approach Krasus. Menachem bows, greets him and says: "Good morning, sir. This young man comes from a distant village near Beirut. He desires to buy a Hebrew maidservant here. Perhaps my lord will be good enough to sell him one of the girls working in your workshop?"

Krasus studies the old man and the young fellow with his black eyes, and says: "Why do you come to me? Aren't such goods to be purchased in the marketplace?"

The old man responds: "We have already been to the market, and the young son of my master did not find one to his liking."

"Generally I refuse to sell my maidservants, but now that sales have declined, if you pay her worth, maybe I'll do you a favor. Follow me."

He leads them through many storerooms, packed full of carpets and rugs, and storerooms of raw materials—bundles of wool, and dyes, and other things—until at last they come to a yard, which they cross to enter a large lofty building. On the floor, sitting or standing, are more than a hundred girls and women at work. Some are weaving; some embroidering; others spin, or sew. Each woman has her task. As they enter, the workers raise their eyes, look at the visitors and a whisper rustles among them.

"They are of all nations and races. There are only three Hebrews. After the fall of Judah, there were more. They were diligent and learned the more delicate work, but a few Jewish merchants who buy carpets from me came and urged me to sell them. Of these three, one is an old woman. Most certainly, your master will not want to buy her," says

Krasus with a smile, "and of the two young ones, there is one whom I bought six years ago. Now she is about sixteen, of pleasing appearance, one of my expert workers in colored carpets. This one I will not sell, even if you weigh up three hundred shekels of silver. There she is, in the corner. She has long plaits. But I have another, whom I bought a year ago. She is by no means ugly, and her work is not bad. I may be persuaded to sell her."

With his visitors, he approaches one of the corners, and there sits a young girl of about nineteen, graceful and pleasing. Her face is sad. She raises her eyes, and drops them in confusion, as a blush spreads over her cheeks. But Avshalom and Menachem turn to look at the girl with the plaits who sits at a distance of five paces from them, bent over a large carpet where she works with her fingers racing at great speed.

Avshalom's heart thumps.

Rachel. . . . His eyes sparkle with anger and excitement simultaneously. . . . She is his friend. She is his. Who is entitled to make her a slave? But he restrains himself. He stands as though turned to stone. Menachem glances up at Avshalom, reads what is taking place in his heart, squeezes his hand to calm him and whispers: "Don't get excited. They'll see your emotion and increase the price. Be composed and don't dare to go near her."

Krasus meanwhile goes up to a few of the workers, examines their work, makes some comment, and then he comes back to the two.

"I admit that on the slave market, a girl like this would cost you less. But I will not take less than sixty silver shekels for her. All this year, I have not earned anything through her. She has just been an apprentice. Now she is worth a good deal to me."

"My highly esteemed master: this girl does not find favor in my master's eyes. He likes that one better–with the plaits."

In a dry cutting voice, Krasus states: "That one I will not hand over to you even for three hundred. She is one of the three most expert craftswomen in my whole shop."

"My lord, we'll add a few more shekels, and take her."

"No. I'll never sell her."

He turns and leads them out of the workshop, with the two following in despair and completely at a loss. Avshalom's knees are weak.

In silence and with sorrow, they return to the tavern at Eli's. When Nafthali and Gideon hear all this, they too are downcast.

This is their third day in Damascus, and they have not accomplished anything so far. Despairing and depressed, the four of them sit down to eat their poor repast.

28

"What now?"

Avshalom rouses himself as though from a coma. The question cuts through the empty space of the room and is lost without answer.

Gideon pleads: "Let us go to look for Father."

"Yes, my son. Let us go to the village Ein-Shemesh. It is a distance of five hours on foot. If we leave immediately, we shall reach it at sunset. The asses have rested and the pace will be fast."

"Are you sure Yehudah is there?"

"A year ago he was. Something may have happened meanwhile."

It does not take many minutes and the asses are strapped: the riders take leave of Eli, and turn northward, bound for the village of Ein-Shemesh.

On the way, Nafthali inquires: "How much did Krasus want for the other girl?"

"Sixty silver shekels."

"And for Rachel he said he would not take even three hundred? Had he agreed to sell her for sixty shekels, where would we have got the money? The whole amount we have with us is one hundred and ten shekels. And we have spent a good deal on clothes, and the ransom for Yehudah will certainly be no mean sum."

"You are right, Nafthali. If Krasus had said that he wanted one hundred shekels for Rachel, we would have weighed it out at once, and who knows what would have been Yehudah's fate?"

Menachem whispers as if to himself: "God on High will be our help, my sons."

At sunset, they arrive at the village Ein-Shemesh. It is a large cultivated village, with lovely gardens everywhere. On the slopes of the village, on a high hill, stands a beautiful palace amidst fir and cedar trees, the whole surrounded by a stone wall. In this palace lives the nobleman, Pilatus.

When they reach the wall, the gates are closed. No one comes out and no one goes in. They wait and wait, in the hope that one of the slaves of the officer will appear, but no one comes.

"We'll sleep in the village, and early tomorrow, we'll take up our stand some distance from the gate. We'll ask the slaves where Yehudah works. Maybe he himself will be seen going to work in one of the orchards."

With the morning, the four visitors do indeed take up

their stand on the road, some distance from the back gate through which the slaves come out.

The slaves stream out, tens and tens of them, with spades and hoes on their shoulders. Among them are young men, their clothes torn and patched, their faces thin and lined. Wretched souls. There are some who come out with their feet in chains, and with spades on their shoulders. Yehudah is not to be seen. Menachem approaches the slaves one after another. No one knows anything about Yehudah.

"There is no one like that amongst us."

Menachem does not stop asking. In the end, he comes across an old slave, whose clothing is slightly better. Apparently, he is an overseer of the laborers. He asks him too.

"Ah, yes, Yehudah the Shibbolite? Yes, I knew him. A man of rebellion and anger. A first-class worker, but he refuses to submit to authority. Once he almost killed one of the overseers. He tried twice to escape, and was caught. In the end, my master sent him to the marble quarries in the mountains."

"Is the place far from here?"

The slave raises his eyes and points his hand eastward toward the mountains.

"Over there. Do you see the peak of the mountain? From here, it takes about three hours to get there."

"Do they let one enter?"

"No. Entrance is strictly forbidden. The camp is surrounded by a stone wall. Most of the men are chained. Sentries and watchmen stand on guard before the wall day and night."

"Why such heavy precautions?"

"Because these particular slaves are very difficult, rebellious, insolent . . ."

"Is it possible to redeem someone with money?"

"It certainly is, but the process is very exhausting. The person in charge is only the overseer of these slaves. He is forbidden to sell slaves or liberate them. As for the owners of the quarry, some of them live in Damascus, and some in Rome."

"Is there a village near the quarry where one can lodge?"

"Yes, there is a little village at the foot of the mountain."

Menachem thanks the slave for his information, and goes back to his friends.

"It is bad. Yehudah is not here. He works in the stone quarries in those mountains, three hours from here. He is in chains all the time."

Little Gideon's eyes blaze.

"Let us go at once to the mountains to liberate him!" he demands.

"Of course we'll go. Do you think we'll leave him, Gideon?"

They ride on toward the mountains.

When they get to the top of one of the high peaks, they can see in the distance a tremendous deep quarry. They can make out people bent over their work, one with a huge mallet, another with an iron ax, yet another with a hewing implement. It is difficult to distinguish between one man and another. They resemble a tangled skein of wool. Around the quarry stand the guards armed with swords and keeping a sharp lookout.

The travelers dismount at the little village where they are to lodge, and start a conversation with the villagers about the quarry. One farmer explains: "It will take twenty-five years to exhaust this quarry. It is a treasure trove indeed. If you want beautiful stone, you can obtain it here, especially reddish marble, a lovely sight. The workers are slaves, who are criminals, sinners, evil-doers. It is a sort of prison."

"Is no one from outside permitted to go in?"

"What for? There are some prisoners who are quiet and do not resist. The spirit of rebellion has abated in them. These are permitted to see relatives and visitors. Of course, when they go out to see relatives, they are fettered, with guards at their sides."

"Do you ever go in to see them?"

"We are not strangers that entrance should be forbidden us. On the contrary, at times we come to them and sell them odds and ends. But since most of them are poor, purchases are very few, so that we don't go except at long intervals."

When Menachem hears this, he plans to send a note to Yehudah with one of the village inhabitants, and when he goes to bed he is still thinking it over. Gideon, although very tired, cannot fall asleep. Lying on his back, his eyes wide open, he thinks about his father on the other side of that wall. Each time he remembers how short the distance is between him and his father, a shiver passes through his limbs. A daring thought dazzles him. That very night he will cross the wall secretly, find his father, see him and talk to him. If he cannot set him free, he will go to the overseers and say to them: "I'll be a slave here instead of my father!"

He gets up, looks about. His companions are sleeping heavily. The village is silent. Softly, stepping carefully, he leaves the village, climbs the mountain, makes his way around to the other side and finds himself about one hundred paces from the wall. The going is difficult. With every step, he strikes rocks and stones. But these rocks also offer a hiding place from the sentinels on the wall. The moon sinks slowly down, and will soon vanish. Then darkness will cover everything. He crawls a few steps, hides behind a rock, and listens. Silence. A few more steps and once again he hides and listens. About ten steps from the wall, he comes to sharp, protruding rocks. He hides behind one and examines the wall. It is about one hundred steps long, and only one guard is marching along the top. Every now and then he stops. He sits down on a rock, facing inward.

Still by the light of the sinking moon, Gideon sees that to his right the earth comes up higher, thus making the height of the wall somewhat less at that point. Stealthily, he crawls to the right and hides about five steps from the wall. He waits until the guard has completed his beat on the wall, and has sat down. Gideon notes that the interval before the sentry resumes marching is about a quarter of an hour. Two stones that are near the wall will be of help. As the moon sinks, and the guard marches past and sits down, Gideon approaches the wall, rolling one stone nearer the wall. He brings the other and places it on the first. But as he lifts a third smaller stone, he hears the steps of the guard. Gideon crouches at the foot of the wall, and when the guard sits down again, he places the third stone on top of the other two. He tries standing on them, but they are unsteady. He gets off, scratches up earth with his hands and packs it between the stones.

When he stands on them this time, he hears the guard's steps again. Gideon holds his breath, waiting for the guard to pass. Then he gets up, grabs hold of a stone protruding from the wall, lifts his legs like a cat, pulls himself up, and finds himself on the wall. He lies flat, breathing deeply, while he scans the darkness for a spot to which he can jump. At that moment, the guard who has reached the end of his beat, meets the guard marching on the left wall. The two begin to chat.

Gideon, although he does not know how high it is, throws himself down on the inside of the wall. Luckily, he falls on a place where there is no iron nor stone nor anything hard or sharp that can kill him. But for some moments he lies almost unconscious, and, when he comes to, his thigh and his left leg hurt. A groan escapes him involuntarily, but he controls himself with all his might so as not to groan again.

The guard passes on the wall, and does not notice a small heap crouching down below at the bottom of the wall. For about ten minutes Gideon lies there, not knowing how he can continue to crawl while suffering such pain. He begins to creep like an animal. He crawls and listens. In the middle of the big yard, by the pale light of the stars, his sharp eyes can make out tents and huts. Silence. It is obvious that the slaves are asleep, tired out from their hard labor.

He sees an open tent—approaches, and is greeted by a loud snore. He goes to another tent—again a snore. All the time he keeps asking himself: How will he find his father among all these tens and tens of tents and huts? If he makes a noise, he'll be caught as a criminal, and his father will be punished with lashes or even murder. His heart twists with remorse and pain for what he has done. He thinks: "Better to return." But how can he when the wall is so high on the inside and his whole body aches?

Near one of the tents, he comes across a barrel of water. He cannot find anything to drink from so he puts his head into it and sips. Then he sits near the barrel, feeling restored by the water. He looks at the stars and thinks: it is only midnight now. He crawls between the tents. Next to one hut, he stops. He hears a cough. A man turns over on his side. He says something. Gideon comes to the door of the open hut, crouches beside it and thinks. What should he do? The man who coughed comes out to drink water. He passes next to Gideon without noticing anything. He has a drink and returns. At the entrance to the hut, Gideon takes hold of his leg and whispers: "Sh . . . sh . . . Listen . . ."

Scared, the man pulls his foot away and asks: "Who is there?"

"Sh . . . sh . . . Listen . . . here . . ."

The man bends down and asks in a whisper. "Who are you?"

"I am a child. Tell me please . . ."

"A child? Yes. Now I can see that you are a child. Who are you and what do you want?"

"I am looking for my father."

"Your father! Who is he?"

"Swear you won't tell them about him—and me. Swear!"

"Little fool. In camp no one tells tales. We are all slaves together. You can trust me."

Whispering right into his ear, Gideon says: "Yehudah, the Shibbolite. A Hebrew."

"Ah . . . Yehudah the Shibbolite. Are you his son? He thinks about you day and night . . . Follow me."

"Must I crawl?"

"No. Inside the camp you can walk and make a noise. The guards don't pay attention to movement and noise and talking, and they won't see anything because of the darkness. Your shadow is like the shadow of any slave."

The two walk about fifteen paces. The man tells Gideon to wait in an empty hut. He goes on. Under one of the tents, he bends down, pulls the leg of a sleeping man and whispers to him: "Come out, come out."

"Who is it?" asks a sleepy, hoarse voice.

"Come out, I tell you. Don't make a noise."

From the entrance of the tent a man comes out, tall, erect, chains clanging on his legs.

He remarks: "Oh, it's you, Zidoni."

"Yes. It's I. Follow me."

They pass between the tents, come to an empty hut, and then Zidoni whispers: "Sit down."

"Is there someone else with us?"

"In a moment you'll know."

They sit down.

Gideon is confused. His heart thumps like a hammer.

"Listen, Yehudah. A visitor has come to you. A visitor from Vale-of-Figs."

"To me? Who is it?" He turns to Gideon, crouching in the dark. "Who are you?"

Zidoni says: "Control yourself."

He is still talking when Gideon jumps on Yehudah's lap, and weeping and sobbing, bursts out: "Father!"

"Gideon!" A roar breaks from Yehudah's mouth.

"Yes. This is your son, Yehudah. I told you to control yourself."

Gideon stammers out his story, in fragments.

The Shibbolite asks: "Weren't you hurt when you jumped from the wall?"

"My leg and my knee were injured a bit."

"Is it very painful?"

"No."

Yehudah is very moved. He cannot cease embracing and kissing his son. He cries like a child. Then he controls himself and forces himself to listen quietly. Suddenly, he looks at the stars and says, worried: "In another hour, day will break. Time is short. You must leave the camp. If you don't, you will place both yourself and me in danger. It is harder to get out of here than to get in, and we had better be doubly careful. I know a place from which you can get out. Give Avshalom and Nafthali my blessing, and tell Avshalom his parents are in a village two hours from Damascus on the road to Tiberias. I have not been there, but I know its name. Ein-Selah. They hired a small piece of land outside the village and built a hut on it. Their situation is difficult, and they eke out a poor living. There is something else you must tell Menachem. Do not redeem me. It is not necessary. I have escaped several times, and been caught. I'll run away again soon. If I had only known that you were alive, my strength would have been multiplied sevenfold. I would have destroyed and smashed all that stood in my way to bedevil me.

"You can help me with one thing only. I was recaptured because I could not get away when I was out of the camp. That is the hardest part. Half-an-hour's distance from here, going east, there is an old abandoned quarry. In its deepest side, there is a sort of depression in the wall that looks like a small cave. Leave a change of clothes for me there, the clothes of a Roman soldier, preferably an officer's uniform. I'll never be recaptured wearing that. I'll change into the clothes and immediately head for Avshalom's father Abraham, the Azati. You can wait for me there. From there . . . we'll go on . . . Do you understand, Gideon, my boy?"

"I understand. We'll do everything exactly as you say."

Suddenly Gideon's face clouds over. He asks fearfully: "What if they capture you? Shouldn't we rather redeem you with money?"

"You will need the money to redeem Rachel. Rely on me, on your father. And now, dear boy, follow me."

The three of them stand up. Very quietly, and with extreme caution, they approach the wall. Zidoni hurries away and brings a thick straw mattress. They listen to the footsteps of the guard, and when he has marched off, Yehudah stands on the sack of straw. Gideon climbs on him and stands on his shoulders. Yehudah stretches his two arms upward as far as he can reach. Gideon stands on the palms of his hands. He takes hold of the wall and heaves himself up. On the top, he lies flat for a while, then takes a few steps to the right, so as to be above the point where the ground is lowest as Yehudah has instructed him, and jumps.

Just before dawn, Gideon arrives back at the village. He steals over the threshing floor, finds his companions, crawls over to them, and finds them sleeping heavily, snoring. He too lies down on the straw, as if sleeping, but cannot restrain his feelings, and arouses Menachem. The others wake up as well, and he tells them of his exploits. Then Menachem says: "That was a good dream, Gideon. Now, lie down and go to sleep."

Only after he repeats the story a second time with all its details, shows them his injuries, and tells them the name of the place where Avshalom's parents are, does Avshalom say: "It is not a dream! It's the truth!"

Nafthali puts his arms around Gideon in a brotherly embrace. "The blood of your father flows in your veins," he comments. "May you go from strength to strength!"

29

They realize that every moment is precious. As the sun rises, they mount their asses. At noon, they enter the gates of Damascus. In the market they buy presents for Avshalom's parents. By sunset, they have already reached Ein-Selah. The village lies perched on a peak, but fifty paces from it there are vegetable gardens, fruit orchards, vineyards. A passerby tells them where Avshalom's parents dwell. Between two orchards there is a small plot of land, in size about a day and a half of plowing with oxen. On half the plot grow fruit trees and vines, and on the other half, vegetables. In the yard there is a small house made of clay, like a low hut, with a furrow of water running past, which waters the garden.

First Menachem goes in. He finds Abraham sitting in front of his hut, mending a wicker basket for carrying vegetables to the city. The boys wait some distance away, behind one of the trees, so that they cannot be seen.

"Peace be unto you, my friend Abraham," says Menachem in a shaking voice.

"May your coming within the shadow of my hut be in peace, my friend Menachem." The old man gets up, his hands extended in affection. "Sit down. Where do you come from and what have you been doing?"

"From roaming the world, a wanderer."

"What news from there?"

"The desert is not awakening to a rebirth. There is mourning and suffering and desolation throughout the land. Only from Galilee are there good tidings. King Agrippa rules Galilee by the grace of the Romans."

"That traitor! Will you draw honey from a viper?" exclaims Abraham angrily.

"Calm down, my friend. Agrippa has repented of his deeds. He deals kindly with his countrymen, tries to help . . ."

So the two converse and the boys outside listen, their hearts thumping in anticipation.

Abraham raises his voice and calls into the inner court: "Miriam! Come here Miriam!" Steps are heard behind the hut. From afar, Miriam asks worriedly: "What is the matter, Abraham?"

"An important guest has come to us, Menachem."

"Oh, Menachem," Miriam cries. "It is so long since we have seen one of our own people. Each one has his own suffering. Each one mourns." And she sighs a deep sigh. She inquires after Menachem's health and then says: "What have you heard about the rest of the exiles? One by one they are disappearing. Woe is us!"

"Miriam, Menachem is surely hungry and thirsty. Will you prepare some food."

"Please do not worry," says Menachem: "I ate before I left Damascus. Sit down and I'll tell you some good news. This is why I have come."

They all sit down. In the evening twilight, Menachem begins his tale, choosing his words carefully so as not to frighten them.

"Our children are alive. Your Avshalom is strong and well. A youth like a cedar. My Miriam, too, is alive . . . a beautiful girl. The rest of the children from the cave are all alive."

Miriam bursts out in a voice quite unlike her own: "Menachem! Are you telling the truth? Oh, God! How can I ever thank Thee if my Avshalom is still alive?"

Abraham seizes Menachem's hand and says in a trembling voice: "Swear to me, Menachem. Are you telling the truth?"

Menachem, too, is very moved and answers: "I swear by God. They are alive and well."

"But Rachel told us that our son Avshalom was killed by the Roman who took her captive?"

"He fell in a faint, wounded. But he recovered."

"Who told you all this?"

"I saw them with my own eyes."

"Really? Have you been there, in the Hills of Ephraim?"

"I was in our village. Your Avshalom is a strong, handsome young man. I saw the son of Yehudah the Shibbolite, also. Today he is brave, full of fun, a fine boy. Just like his father."

"They are alive?"

"All of them."

"How do they live, these poor orphans?"

Menachem related in detail about their lives and how they lived and ended by saying: "They are all one big family. They have done away with 'yours' and 'mine.' They are loyal and devoted to each other."

Miriam shakes herself as though out of a pleasant sweet sleep or from a happy dream, and asks again with great joy: "So our son Avshalom is alive?"

"Alive, alive."

"What message did he send us?"

"He wants you to come home."

"Oh, we shall return! Of course, we shall return! Even though I am rather feeble and Abraham is weak, too. With song and dance, we shall return to our village, to our children." Suddenly she bursts into tears, from happiness and relief. She cries, "Oh, our son Avshalom is alive, alive, alive! If only I could kiss you, press you to my heart. How good it would be. Oh, Avshalom! Avshalom!"

Then Menachem turns to her as though joking: "Are you really impatient and would you like to see him immediately?"

"I would give a year of my life to see him now, alive and well."

Menachem raises his hand and declares: "He is here!"

Avshalom leaps forward like a young lion.

"Mother! Father!"

He falls on his knees and embraces his mother. His father comes over to him and hugs him. And so the three embrace, weeping with excitement. Nafthali and Gideon also come and sit next to Menachem and watch with joy the happiness of the parents with their son.

30

At the end of a very happy day, Nafthali remarks: "Avshalom and Gideon, you both remain here. Menachem and I must return to Damascus to obtain the uniform of a Roman officer for Yehudah."

"I'll go with you," says Gideon.

"Why? You're hurt. You'll drag along for nothing. Stay here and rest."

"What about Rachel?" asks Avshalom anxiously.

"In Damascus, we'll see Yoram and discuss the matter with him."

So Menachem and Nafthali return to Damascus. They look around the market for a soldier's uniform. They visit several tailors and see many uniforms but these are too small for Yehudah's great height and girth. Finally, in one of the stalls, they find a uniform of a Roman officer, together with a beautiful sword.

"We'll buy this, and the sword too," says Nafthali.

"I don't understand why we must take an officer's scarlet uniform and a sword."

"Surely Yehudah knows."

"Very well. If it is not too expensive, we'll buy it."

They bargain: they go and come back time and again, until at last the uniform is bought and packed into a parcel. On their way to the quarry, Nafthali says to Menachem: "I have an idea."

"What is it?"

"Let us put a purse in one of the pockets, with ten silver shekels in it. If he escapes, he won't have a single coin. He may be in danger, and this money may come in useful as bribes, perhaps."

"That is really a good idea."

They hide the parcel in the small cave of the ancient quarry and then return.

The next day they call on Yoram from the carpet shop. He is loathe to be seen with them in a public tavern, so they sit in one of the city gardens in the shade of the trees.

He says: "My master is not willing to sell Rachel, not even for a huge amount of silver and gold."

"What shall we do?"

Yoram shrugs his shoulders and sighs: "All I can tell you is that Krasus is leaving for Rome in five days in connection with his trade. Then the supervision in the workshop is relaxed somewhat. Now, do whatever you think right."

"Many thanks, Yoram, for your advice. But what can we do?"

"I really do not know." And so saying, he leaves them.

For a few days, they hover about in the vicinity of the workshop. They look at the high wall and wonder how to kidnap a girl from such a fortress, in a teeming city, with soldiers everywhere. They are at their wits' end.

Ten days pass since the night Gideon jumped over the wall, and still Yehudah does not come. Each night they wait, listening for his footsteps. Maybe . . . maybe . . . and each night they are disappointed.

Eventually, they decide to see if the clothes are still in the cave. Nafthali goes alone. To his great surprise, he finds the clothes still lying there, a sign that Yehudah has not yet escaped. Then it occurs to him that he should let Yehudah know about Rachel. With his knife, he scratches these words on a soft smooth stone. "R. not for sale. Krasus gone to Rome. We are in a dilemma." And he leaves the stone with the uniform.

31

One fine day, a couple of hours before sunset, a Roman officer rides up on his horse and stops at the door of Krasus' shop. It is obvious from his uniform, his commanding presence and his decorations that he is a distinguished senior officer. The shop assistants, headed by the manager, who is deputizing for Krasus, hurry out and bow obsequiously.

"Is this the workshop of my friend Krasus?"

"Yes, your Excellency."

He dismounts, hands the reins to the assistants, and with lofty bearing, enters the shop. The manager pulls up the soft leather seat that stands at the cash table and begs him to sit down, while he, with extreme politeness, awaits his pleasure. The other assistants disappear into corners of the shop and watch from a respectful distance.

The officer announces in polished Latin: "Two days ago I met Krasus. I gave him a letter of recommendation to one of my acquaintances in the Emperor's court, who wants to purchase some very good carpets."

"A thousand thanks to your highly esteemed Excellency," breathes the manager, salaaming deeply.

"But I am worried in case you people cheat him. If I give Krasus a letter of recommendation and I find that you supply poor, cheap, inferior carpets, I will make you sorry you were born!" roars the officer suddenly, in a mighty voice.

The manager turns pale and stammers, bowing and scraping:

"I swear to his high Excellency that only the finest carpets in the world will be sent!"

"Beware!" storms the officer again. "Just as I can open doors for your master in Caesar's court so that he can make a fortune of thousands of drachmas, so can I have him thrown into prison and destroy this place and all of you with it!"

"Why is our most gracious lord angry with us, when all the world knows we are honest merchants who never stoop to fraud or deceit?"

"Next, a further matter. Krasus, your master, promised me a gift, one of his lovely maidens. There is, in his workshop, he told me, a Hebrew girl—her name is Rachel—whom he described as very beautiful. She has long plaits. I want no presents, but while I am in Damascus, I want this girl to serve me. I'll stay here no longer than one month."

The manager is perplexed, knowing how precious this

girl is to her master. However, when he considers that the period is for one month only, he feels more at ease, and says in an ingratiating voice: "Certainly, most exalted Excellency. In our workshop there is such a girl, indeed the most beautiful of all girls. I am sure my master would do anything to please your Excellency. I shall send this girl to you."

The officer stands up and says: "Bring her to me at my inn, Caesar's Beacon, within half an hour. Do not bother to change her garments. I have already ordered silks for her. And do not tell her where you are taking her. Do you hear?" He raises his voice again. "These Hebrews are wild and obstinate," he shouts.

So saying, he stalks out, mounts his horse, and gallops away.

Half an hour later, Rachel is brought to the Caesar's Beacon Inn. Two assistants drag her, weeping and pleading, into the inn. They jeer and mock at her, hurling insults and humiliating remarks at her while she weeps bitterly.

Her weeping is of no avail. As the sun sets, she is forced to enter the luxurious inn. The attendants open the door of a room and push her in, still struggling. The officer comes out to Krasus' assistants and puts some silver shekels into their hands. Bowing obsequiously, they leave the inn, highly satisfied.

When the officer returns to the room, he finds the girl crouching on the floor, sobbing, tearing her hair and trembling. He draws near, pats her head and whispers: "Rachel."

She cowers back, like a wounded lioness; then falls at the

feet of the officer and begins to plead, "Have pity on me. Do not touch me. I'll never forget you."

The officer locks the door, looks out of the window to make sure no one is eavesdropping, stoops over her and whispers in the Holy Tongue: "Rachel, don't be afraid. I am here to protect and save you. I am Yehudah the Shibbolite."

Rachel raises her eyes to look at him. Then she falls on her knees and kisses his hands. "Yehudah, save me!"

When she has calmed down, Yehudah makes her drink a little date juice. Then he says: "Every moment is precious. We must flee. I too have escaped, and with us, there will be several others who are running away. I'll tell you everything on the way. Now, put on this dress, cover your face with a veil and leave. Wait for me at the western gate. In an hour I'll come riding past and I'll snatch you up onto my horse. We'll race swiftly on our way, home to our Motherland, to Vale-of-Figs."

When she hears these words, she trembles for joy, her eyes sparkling. But he puts his hand to her mouth and whispers: "Hurry. Go."

She changes her clothes, covers her face with the veil and leaves for the western gate. Meanwhile, he calls the innkeeper and says: "Tomorrow my retinue and all my baggage will arrive. You will see to it that all my belongings are placed in safekeeping. This room is to be reserved for me. I will return in two days."

He jumps on his horse and canters through the thronging streets of Damascus. In the hustle and bustle of the early evening, he finds Rachel at the western gate, bends and sweeps her up onto his horse.

About two and a half hours later, a Roman officer with a girl sitting behind him, holding onto him, arrives at the vegetable field. He jumps off the horse, and Abraham, father of Avshalom, comes out to greet him. Abraham is very much afraid of this man in the uniform of a senior army officer. His legs totter and he stutters as he asks: "How can I serve your Excellency?"

Yehudah replies in the Holy Tongue: "Rachel is with me."

Avshalom, who with the others, is standing by, cries, his heart bursting: "Rachel!"

And the others, too, cry, "Rachel, where?"

Yehudah leaps down from the horse, and with his strong arms, lifts Rachel down as if she were a feather.

"Rachel, your friends Avshalom and Nafthali, and my son, Gideon, are all here."

Rachel runs to Avshalom and falls into his arms, murmuring "Avshalom, Avshalom."

At that moment, Yehudah lifts Gideon in his arms, embraces him and kisses him by turns.

"Father! It's you!"

"Yes. Here I am, a Roman officer all of a sudden!"

"Will you be a Jewish officer in our country?"

"Please God! When He raises the tottering Tabernacle of Judah once more."

Then as Yehudah puts Gideon down, he calls for quiet, and says in an authoritative voice:

"We have five minutes at our disposal. Rachel and I must hurry, being fugitives. We shall ride away immediately. You too must leave within an hour on your donkeys. We shall wait for you at the pool at Mei-Merom."

He puts Rachel, pale with excitement, back on the horse. Then he mounts and calls farewell, and they gallop away.

32

Vale-of-Figs. The month of Tishrei. It is evening, moonlit and bright. After the day's work of harvesting olives, the boys and girls are sitting on the flat roof of the new house chatting.

"It's five weeks since they left, and they haven't returned yet."

"Something must have happened to them," says Miriam sadly.

"Yes. We thought they would take ten days, or two weeks, and now . . ." Elchanan worries.

"Maybe they went to Egypt," remarks the youngest of the group.

They all burst out laughing, and Dinah says: "Damascus is northeast and Egypt is south."

"And I think," says Bruria, "that just because they're

taking a long time, that means good news. Maybe they found traces of other captives and exiles."

"We decided then that they should not go to Rome. So why this delay?"

"Of course they didn't go anywhere except to Damascus, and that is why it is a puzzle. Perhaps someone was ill on the way, or thrown into prison . . ."

"Whatever for?"

"And I say," says Miriam, "if they don't come back within a week, two of us must be sent to find out what has happened. Perhaps they need help."

"This time I shall go," says Yochanan.

"And I too," Gedaliah puts in.

So the family sit on the roof and discuss their worries.

Suddenly they hear a noise. They prick up their ears and listen, listen. Someone murmurs: "Riders."

"Coming nearer."

In a flash everyone gets up and rushes to the wall.

They peer out into the night, listening intently. From the slope of the hill opposite, the sounds are approaching.

"Maybe they're enemies. Maybe robbers."

"Take good care, everyone. The gate is closed, of course?"

"Yes, I closed it."

"I think," says Bruria, "they're our people."

Breathless silence. Again someone breathes the question: "Is the gate closed?"

The noises come nearer, nearer, then right up to the wall. Into the silence of expectation and fear, penetrates a strong, clear voice from the gate below.

"Open the gate. We have come home!"

Trembling with relief and taut with excitement, like arrows from a bow, they all shoot down the steps. The gate is opened. The moon witnesses a meeting so joyous that no words and no pen can describe it.

When they ascend into the spacious hall, Yehudah sees the palace built by the hands of the children. Then, when from the rooftop he looks out by the light of the moon over the green gardens of Vale-of-Figs, a wave of warmth suffuses his inner being. Tears fill his eyes. In a loud but tender tone, he says:

"My children, and my brothers and sisters! There is a time for everything: a time to weep and a time to laugh; a time to revolt and destroy, and a time to rebuild the ruins, to collect stones that have fallen and to erect a new building, to plant trees, to sow; a time to slay on the battlefields, and a time to renew the covenant with the soil. I have been a Zealot, a rebel; I have shed my blood for the freedom of our people and our land. I was regarded as a hero, but you, my children, have done greater deeds than I. You have sowed the seeds of the new Motherland . . ."

Overwhelmed by emotion, Yehudah sheds tears of joy, and the whole family rejoices with him.